Catherynne M. Valente

SIX-GUN
SNOW WHITE

SIX-GUN
SNOW WHITE

Catherynne M. Valente

SUBTERRANEAN PRESS • 2013

First Edition

ISBN
978-1-59606-552-9

Subterranean Press
PO Box 190106
Burton, MI 48519

www.subterraneanpress.com

Coyote had a plan
which he knew he
could carry out because
of his great power. He
took his heart and cut it
in half. He put one half
right at the tip of his
nose and the other half
at the end of his tail.

——APACHE FOLKTALE

PART I

How Snow White
Got Her Cunning

The Creation of
Snow White

I **accept with equanimity** that you will not credit me when I tell you Mr. H married a Crow woman and had a baby with her round about the time he struck his fortune in the good blue, which is how folk used to designate Nevada silver. It don't trouble me none if any soul calls me a liar.

The biography of Mr. H is well known: he had one wife and one son and that was the beginning and the end of his capacity for love, excepting of course the copper lode in Peru, gold prospects in the Dakota Territories, the Idaho opal mine, and other pursuits I cannot tell you about as they are beyond my ken. Most everyone grants he was a kingly fellow, else the blue would not have showed itself to him. That is a wholly peculiar way of thinking, but it is very common.

This is the truth of it:

Flush and jangle with silver and possessed of a powerful tooth for both spending and procuring more of whatever glittered under the ground, Mr. H traveled to the Montana

Territory on a horse so new and fine her tail squeaked. He disliked to travel in company, being a secretive man by nature. Mr. H had a witch's own knack for sniffing out what the earth had to give up. The notion of a sapphire rush brewing in the Beartooth Range pricked up the north of that comstock-compass stuck in his heart. All the way out in San Francisco he felt the rumble of the shine. However, upon his arrival in Billings and establishment at the Bear Gulch Hotel, the whiskeytalk leaned another way: black diamonds. That is how coal miners appellate their livelihood. In my experience, folk find it nigh on impossible to call a thing what it is.

It never mattered much to Mr. H whether silver or sapphires or coal or copper weighed his pockets just so long as he never walked empty. He made his arrangements to accompany a pair of Cornishmen into the range the next morning. He strode out into the bone-cracking cold to survey the town, though Billings in those days could barely be called more than a camp. Horseshit outnumbered honest men by a margin.

Mr. H encountered the woman who would be his first wife by chance alone. She turned up like an ace of spades in the general store, trading elk meat for cotton cloth and buttons. Her brother, who had shot the beast, escorted her. But the girl did the bargaining. She had good English and did not like the owner of the general store.

The terrible covetous heart of Mr. H immediately conceived a starvation for the girl not lesser in might than his thirst for sapphires or gold. In the lamplight her hair had the very color of coal, plaited in two long braids and swept up at the brow into what I have heard called a pompadour. Her dark mouth was a cut garnet, her skin rich copper, her eyes black diamonds for true. She looked over her shoulder at him and her body hardened to run if such became necessary. Mr. H took this slight stiffening as a sign that his feeling was returned. He saw no reason any person should fear him, being well-dressed and pleasant enough in his features. He had loved women already in his time, though never married, all of them of good though not old family. Square-shouldered sunburned freckles and kisses like milk and hair brushed a hundred times before bed. He savored a rich seam of shame over his lust for the Crow woman and this shame made him only more needful.

Mr. H purposed himself to have her. He inquired after her name, her family, how often she visited the town to trade, where she and hers might make their camp. The Beartooth coal ran thick and deep, but he did his business by rote. Mr. H had sung his song many times. It sang itself. His true occupation was now the striking of the Crow woman, whose name was Gun That Sings. At first, his imagination wakened only to the possibility of bedding her. He saw no reason this should not be possible and right quick. Silver speaks louder than sin. But when Gun That Sings returned to town with her relations and Mr. H had opportunity to clap eyes on her again, he knew he could not be satisfied except to own her entirely. A man don't rent a silver mine. He buys it right out.

He attired himself in a fine new suit sent by coach from San Francisco along with jewelry, gowns, and other items indicating his affection, for he was prepared to make her a civilized woman. He would put silk on her body and emerald combs in her hair. He would teach her to read Shakespeare and encourage her to play out the part of wild Titania in his parlor at home, naked save for a belt of violets. He would instruct her in the saying of the Lord's Prayer and the keeping of the Sabbath; he would deliver to heaven a sterling modest maid. The anticipation of transforming her inspired a pleasure so sharp that Mr. H necessitated an entire afternoon to recover from it.

When Mr. H deemed the great moment of his matrimonials to have drawn close, he rode out on his combed and curried horse across the Bighorn River to the village of Gun That Sings's people. Mr. H had often purchased meat and horses from Indians at what he considered a fair price and foresaw no trouble. The card-men at the Bear Gulch Hotel had informed him that the Crow allow their women to rule like heathen Cleopatras, and so Mr. H addressed himself to an old and august lady he spied leading a horse to pasture, requesting the presence of his bride-to-be.

When Gun That Sings was produced, Mr. H suffered some disappointment. She would not look at him, but kept her eyes fixed on the dirt. Her braids caught the winter light and seemed now not only as rich as coal but veined with liquid silver. Mr. H felt a powerful need. He behaved himself as though to a white woman. He presented his prospects to the maiden's mother, his silver mine, his hopes for Dakota, his colleagues in Sacramento, his friends in Washington. As he described himself, the resolve of Mr. H hardened along with his impression of his own endowments, and he lost any doubt that he would be married before the night. Only an addled woman would despise the ring of such an excellent example of frontiersman quality.

I do not know what Gun That Sings said to him. If I had my rather, I would put words in her like bullets. I know she spurned him. That I do know.

Mr. H recovered his pride on the quick. Sometimes a man finds it necessary to work a claim for a space before it gives up the blue. He returned to his rooms to collect the bride gifts that would ensure her. Mr. H chose a gown like the sun to represent him. It sported a high bustle as was the fashion in the city, with sharp pleating at the skirt-hem and a neckline I would not wear if it were stitched in paper money. But the color did not recall the wholesome sun of spring. Its model was instead the terrible inferno of the sun itself, hanging in black space like a Utah ruby, erupting into eternity, pocked with lava.

Once again, Mr. H rode out past the river and presented the baleful dress to Gun That Sings. She looked on it and began to shake in her shoes. Mr. H pressed the gown upon her but she wept bitterly into the cloth and said to her mother: "These are white woman's clothes. Put them in the river; I will burn up inside them."

Mr. H brought next a gown like the moon. This one presented a wasp waist and high lace collar. So much fabric in that skirt it bent a back to lift it over its skeleton-hoop of leather and wire. The shimmer of it took after the moon itself, hard and without poetry, stuck in the orbit of the thoughtless earth like a California pearl. Mr. H lay the dress across the flank of his horse like a stolen girl and forded the Bighorn to lay it out for Gun That Sings. She trembled something fearful and tore the brocade wrestling herself free. She said to her mother: "These are clothes for a white woman. Give them to a white woman. Put them in the fire; I will choke on them."

Mr. H suffered no discouragement for desire speaks louder than decorum. He drew from his trunk a gown like the stars at night. Its long sleeves and gathered skirt were black as Bibles, stitched all over with tiny crystals. In its folds Mr. H concealed a necklace of Colorado diamonds so fine and luxurious anyone who looked at it felt like they were looking at a naked woman, and turned away. The dress of stars glowed with cold, lonely fire, like the Dog Star howling in the black. Mr. H saddled his horse and rode out a third time. When Gun That Sings saw the dress and the necklace she tried to run from it like it was death come for her, but Mr. H caught her up in his arms. He felt a big man with her there, not going anywhere at all. He held her by the throat. He put the necklace on her, all them diamonds hanging down her chest like war medals. Gun That Sings did not cry but stared him down with fury and didn't say a damn thing.

Mr. H didn't let her go for a second. He stood to Gun That Sings' brothers and her mama and her father with his hand on the butt of his gun and told stories about how hitched up he'd got with General This-and-That and Senator Big-Name and wasn't it a nice patch of earth you people have here, right on the river and green as you please. All his Washington friends would just pick up and move right on out here fast as a cough if they could see it. Gun That Sings heard what he had to say and what he didn't say, too, and the next Sunday she stood there in her dress of stars and said her vows and signed her name *Sarah H.* on the register because you can't name a girl for a gun in civilized society.

And I guess that's how a man gets a wife. I've heard it told elsewise but I don't believe it.

Well, Mr. H took his bride to a place he was building, a castle by the sea. He put silk on her body and emerald combs in her hair. He brushed out that hair every night, wrapped himself up in it, drank up the color and heat of coal in it. He kissed her dark blood-bright mouth over and over like he could drink out the color of them too. Mr. H told it with pride that he taught her to read Shakespeare even though she had English letters just fine already. He made her play wild Titania for him wearing nothing at all, not even violets. He instructed her in the saying of the Lord's Prayer and the keeping of the Sabbath and he got her with child.

In his private prayers Mr. H said the following: *let this child have hair like hot coal, and lips bright and dark as blood, but oh Lord, if you're listening, skin as white as mine.*

By now I expect you are shaking your head and tallying up on your fingers the obvious and ungraceful lies of my story. Well, I have told it straight. A body can only deliver up the truth its bones know. Its blood which is its history. My body is my truth, and I have laid it out as evidence on the table of my father's reputation, for by now you may have guessed my next revelation: I was the child Mr. H put inside of Gun That Sings.

Mrs. H uncovered her condition in wintertime. It did not snow much in that part of the country but the ground did freeze, and frost over, and purchase from heaven a meager dusting of the cold stuff. Gun That Sings went out into the forest at night. All the stars like dresses hung up in the sky. She took up a kitchen knife and hacked at her arms until steam rose out of her like she was a kettle. Her blood dripped down onto the white ground and she hoped she'd die but she didn't. Mr. H's people found her and patched her up and locked her in a little room til the baby could come at which point she died anyway, all alone in that big unfinished house.

Snow White
Secures Fire

My father did love me after a kind. He liked to see me trotted out for supper in a lacy white dress, so he could see my black hair against it. He liked to see me dressed in black so my skin looked lighter against that. Less regular, he put me into calf-skin and two long braids which is how Crow girls dress. I did not like the look of him when I did that. Mr. H did not often introduce me to his business acquaintances or his more intimate partners. A daughter was a special doll to be kept in a glass cabinet. An automatic girl the master of the house brought out to entertain at the table with charming words, to be polished up with powder and elaborate costumes. Pull the lever in her heart and she dispenses love, pose her arms and legs and she exhibits grace—then put her away in her cabinet again.

I gradually understood the truth of my situation: I was a secret. Few enough of my father's folk knew he'd married anybody in the first place. Gun That Sings had barely outlived the mail service that delivered their nuptial announcements. Mr. H found it more difficult to explain the sudden appearance of a daughter than to have me privately instructed and forbid me to leave the grounds of the slowly growing castle by the sea.

For a long time this did not trouble me as the grounds would have put the shame to Eden and Babylon. The hills swooped down to the shore in grassy, gentle humps, split up into gardens, fields full of pheasant and grouse for hunting, stables and ponds, good pine forests. Up on the north acreage, my father ordered a tiny zoo built, along with a brass carousel and a miniature boardwalk along the creek. The boardwalk boasted two shooting galleries, a dime museum full of paintings of faraway cities in Europe and South America, and a saloon with a player piano and sarsaparilla taps that never seemed to run dry. Inside the saloon stood a black and silver slot machine specially made to accept wooden coins my father had struck as part of my raising—they pictured myself on one side and Mr. H on the other. I received a set and nonnegotiable number of these every month and could trade them for toys, extra helpings of dessert, another hour before bedtime, or any other sorts of things for which a child might wheedle and beg. The spinners on the slot machine depicted a lonely tree in winter, spring, summer, and autumn. If I lined up the seasons correct, real coins would spill into the tray, silver dollars like raindrops.

I played alone on the boardwalk. My governess was not allowed there as Mr. H felt every soul required a space to lord over. The sun beat my hair and the magpies watched me hopscotch across the birch slats. The slots spun only for me. I pulled my own mugs of sarsaparilla. I shot the tin geese in the galleries over and over again until dark. Sometimes the dime museum paintings changed, but I never saw new canvases hung up or old ones taken down. I had no friends or company other than my father, my governess Miss Enger, and the groundskeeper, who came to feed the animals Mr. H collected on his travels and installed in the zoo. We had an ancient circus bear called Florimond, a red fox, a slow-witted buffalo, a shaggy gibbon's monkey. I was powerful afraid of the crocodile, even though she was caged up. The coyote also lived in a cage, as he could not be trusted to come back if we let him roam like the fox and the bear, who knew a good thing and an easy meal. I recall specially a pair of enormous emerald-colored parrots with red and yellow and purple feathers my father had brought by sea from the West Indies. They could talk a little but they did not speak English.

Mr. H liked more than anything to see me dressed like a boy, with a cattleman's hat and a revolver made to my hand. It had a grip pounded out of the first silver bars of Mr. H's fortune, so pure and bright it could blind a body cold. That would have been gun enough for any girl, but I reckon my father had nowhere else to spend his love back then. He had great big red pearls stuck into it like drops of blood spattered on the snow, one for every time I pleased him. On my tenth birthday he presented me a black opal the size of his thumb which he set himself into the pommel.

Like your mother's eyes, he said. *Like your eyes*, he said.

When I looked at it I did not see my mother's eyes. I saw fire. Veins of fire like anger in the dark. Like coal. Like coals. And in the silver I saw my face reflected like a terrible, wonderful mirror.

I could shoot that gun easy as spitting. The tin gallery-geese, the apples off the orchard trees. I named my gun Rose Red for them fancy cranberries nubbling up against my palm. It was some years before I understood that pearls were more usually white. My main observation on the matter of the opal was that it changed the weight of my gun, which did not please me. If I was not shooting the pea-rifle at tin buffalo on the boardwalk, I spent the better number of my afternoons shooting bottles on my father's high fences, also rabbits, black squirrels, and opossums which I gave to the groundskeeper. He took the meat and returned me the pelts and I judged that a sound bargain. On occasion I shot big black rats which I gave to the coyote, as I do not prefer rat fur. He crunched their skulls between his jaws. He watched me with yellow eyes while he did it. When he howled he sounded like a body dying.

Once, I took a bead on a seagull and shot it plumb out of the sky. I did not expect to come close to it. As soon as it dropped down toward the sea my heart fell through a hole in my chest. I looked for the bird all over the meadowy grass, crying miserable. The sun set my tears to boiling. I talked myself into the notion that I would find the seagull wounded through the wing and keep her and mend her and teach her to love humans and live in a house. She would help me and bring me fish and be my companion. She would sleep in my bed with her soft head against my shoulder.

I found the poor bird down at the bottom of a green hill. I had put my bullet straight through her black eye.

Snow White
Is Instructed By Heron and Lizard

r. H paid wages to these folk, though I am not accounting for the men he employed in San Francisco, Sacramento, Chicago, and New York as I never met them. Most all got some extra scratch for keeping quiet about my person.

Mrs. Maureen Whitney, Housekeeper
Miss Marie Andersen, Kitchen Maid
Miss Annie Dougall, House Maid
Miss Mary Duffy, Laundry Maid
Mrs. Catherine Kenny, Cook
Miss Beatrice Criscone, Scullery Maid
Mr. Thomas Button, Butler
Mr. George Button, Valet
Mr. Simon Paget, Hall Boy
Mr. Garland Clague, Groundskeeper

Mr. Linus Healy, Stablemaster
Mr. Peter Fjelstad, Stablehand
Mr. Henry Fredrik, Useful Man
Miss Christabel Enger, Governess

    I had nursemaids and the like but I do not remember any of them.

Snow White's Father
Replaces Arrows With Bones

I was eleven years of age when Mr. H married the daughter of Mr. M.

The wedding occurred at high summer in the castle by the sea. A whole mess of new people suddenly tramped all over my private kingdom, tying gardenias to every damn thing and building silk tents in the golden grass. The Mr. Buttons were so fussed I thought their heads would fly off and Mrs. Kenny hollered something fierce at the sculleries. The cream was too feared to whip.

The new Mrs. H was a stranger to me. I knew the following interesting items concerning her: Mr. M was a railroad baron and owned most everything Mr. H didn't. She had grown up in Boston and gone to a fancy Paris school for girls. She knew French and Spanish and Latin. Some kind of scandal worried her back east. I heard the wedding people say Mr. H was good to take her after all that business. But I also heard them say the only reason she would marry a man with no family name at all was because of her lowered station.

They all said she was beautiful. It hurt to look at her sometimes, if the wine stewards were to be believed and I did not. Who ever heard of a person so pretty it pinched to set eyes on them? Probably they were drunk, I reasoned.

Mr. H told me to stay out of the way and I did. I stayed in my zoo while the wedding went up like a white circus. I chewed licorice root while the red fox whom I had named Thompson curled in my lap and the big old raggedy bear snored away. *Who, who?* hooted the monkey. *Elle, elle,* answered the emerald parrots together as they did not hold forth separately. I thought on how excited Mr. H got over the idea of a wife. He kept a picture of her in his breast pocket but he would not let me see it. He barely looked at me at dinner, even if I wore my hair in two braids. I did not see the appeal of a wife. We had never had one before. She would not be half as interesting as our buffalo.

Miss Enger said a man required a helpmeet and a solace. She said a house like this cried out for a feminine hand. She said poor Mr. H longed for companionship and children of his own. Two things settled into my brain upon listening to my governess philosophize on the marital condition. The first was that Mr. H had lied upon the matter of me; Miss Enger believed I was his ward and not his daughter. The second was that Miss Enger nurtured hopes concerning my father that had recently been squashed flat. Before Miss Enger my governess had been a Canadian lady called Miss Grace Bornay. She did not think I was anybody's ward. But she and the rest except Mr. Clague the groundskeeper had been let go and new souls brought in a year back. Miss Enger was prettier than Miss Bornay, but Miss Bornay could play the flute and Miss Enger could not so it all came out in the wash.

The fox wandered off into his little fox-house and I walked down to my empty saloon. Maybe the new Mrs. H would sit with me the way the fox did. Maybe she would come to my saloon and play cards around the table where no one else ever upped an ante or called. It might be good fun to play with another body. Maybe she would brush my hair and sing to me and that would be nice. Maybe she liked to shoot. Maybe she would teach me Latin and French and dancing. Maybe she'd want to dress me up as something. Maybe she would love me the way I loved my gun.

I spun the slot machine. Four winter trees whirled up, bare and heavy with ice. A silver dollar rolled into the pan. It echoed a good while.

Snow White
Bites Her Own Reflection

Mrs. H arrived the night before the wedding. A white stagecoach brought her. The inside of the stagecoach was black. I wanted to pick flowers for her and practice a welcome speech. Mr. H told me no. He said I would have plenty of time with her later. I was not to come down or bother her. I was not to bother Mr. M or his servants. I was not to pick flowers for anyone. I was to wait in my room and play with Miss Enger and my toys until the wedding was over, and then Mr. H would figure a way to present me.

I did not apprehend before that moment that Mrs. H did not know Mr. H for a widower with a child already on the ground. She did not think he had a ward, either. She did not know about me at all. If you ask me how I felt on that I will tell you nothing good.

So I watched her come into the house from the window of my bedroom. I hid in the red curtains and peeped down on her. I gathered information. She wore a grey dress with embroidery and white boots. Her hair was braided up nice. It had a color like good whiskey. I could not see her face, only her scalp, white and sharp as a knife. She had what I guess menfolk call a figure. She walked graceful as a grey-hound. Mr. H helped her out of the coach and kissed her cheek. Mr. M bounded out the other side and clapped my father on the shoulder and his piggy jowls shook when he did it. I couldn't hear them talking because my bedroom was very far up. They looked like a puppet show, pumping each other's hands up and down and laughing without making noise.

The new Mrs. H looked up at my window. I am certain she saw me, but I ducked anyway. Her face was shaped like a heart and so pale I thought she might be sick. It did hurt to look at her after all. She looked like a painting that used to hang in my dime museum, with a lady on a shell coming out of the sea. She looked like somebody's mother. But not mine.

It was not customary for a lady to bring her things inside the house while she remained unmarried. They left it all at the servants' doors. Draped with muslin, her trousseau looked like some dreadful machine. I snuck out to look at it while they had a big dinner inside. I could see them through the window. Mr. M drank a bear's measure of wine and his mustache turned red. The new Mrs. H didn't drink at all. She moved her finger around the rim of her glass and didn't sip and watched everyone like a bobcat. Her finger had a ring on it. I knew it was not an engagement ring as it was on her forefinger. It was green, but I did not think it was an emerald. I am only dwelling on her ring because it will be important later. I expect everyone in Boston has something like that ring, which is why I am glad I have never been to Boston.

I took my eyes back from the dinner table on the other side of the window. I lifted the muslin. Underneath it was a chest of linens which I did not find interesting. I walked around the right side of her belongings and lifted the cloth again. I found a chest full of little bottles. Each of them had some different liquid inside it and they smelled something awful. They smelled moldy and damp and also sharp and spicy. They smelled, if you want to know it, like Florimond's pelt after he had gotten rained on. I had on occasion scratched and kissed the old circus bear in the wintertime when he slept very soundly so I am familiar with such smells. As I could not guess what use the bottles might have, I walked around the left side of her belongings and pulled up the drape.

Underneath that was the biggest mirror I ever saw.

It was not like any of the mirrors Mr. H had brought over from Italy and France, with gold all over them and fat babies holding up the corners. It did not have any roses or lilies or ribbons cut out of silver. It was like a door into nothing. The glass did not show the buttery light of the house behind me. It did not show the forest or the meadows. It did not even show me. The glass was so full up of dark it looked like someone had tripped over the night and spilled it all into that mirror. The frame was wood, but wood so old and hard and cold it felt like stone. I reckoned if it came from a tree that tree was the oldest, meanest tree in a forest so secret not even birds knew about it. That tree saw dinosaurs and did not think much of them. I touched the mirror and my fingers went hot and cold, like candles melting.

The moon came on inside the mirror. I could see the craters and the mountains on it clear and true. But the night above my head was moonless as a sack of wool. I dropped the muslin but I did not scream. I do not scream generally or cry very much. But I can run powerful fast.

Snow White
Obtains a Mother

He married her.

I knew I was not to attend the wedding, but I scrapped up a black oak tree and saw the whole thing start to finish. It all happened at sunset under a tent with silver stars painted on it. I never saw so many lanterns or so many flowers. I thought: *nobody else in the whole world must have any roses now.* Mr. H wore a black suit and looked just as fine as rain. A pack of fancy folk arrived in coaches. The ladies wore dresses like springtime and egg whites. The fellows wore velvet and other fabrics I was not aware of. Some of them had long bright guns I would have liked to get a better look at. Little girls and boys threw violet petals on the grass. They were somebody's children, I cannot say whose. I thought to myself that I could throw petals better. The littlest ones dumped half their baskets in one spot. I wanted to throw violets, too. I would throw them so good Mrs. H would give me a kiss.

When the bride came out of the house everybody sighed. She had a dress on all lace and silk like a snowflake and pearls all over her head. Around her neck was a necklace of Colorado diamonds so luxurious I didn't want to look at it, like if I looked at it, I had already stolen it.

After, they danced together. Violins and harps and horns and drums played to wake the moon. Mr. H never stopped smiling. He kissed her seventeen times. I know because I counted. Mr. M danced with a girl in a pink dress and only got two kisses. The violet-tossing children ate too much cake and fell asleep on the grass.

There was a fountain of champagne and it looked like starlight you could drink.

I fell asleep in the black oak tree.

Snow White
and Bobcat
Scratch Each Other

My father and Mrs. H took their honeymoon in Peru where Mr. H intuited the good blue waited for him. I will observe that not even the softness of a bed containing Mrs. H could cool his lechery for silver. The only word I received from them was a painting that appeared in my dime museum. It appeared as suddenly and without warning as if a ghost hung it up. I looked at it a long time. It showed a kind of pyramid with sides like staircases and a flat top. That is how they build pyramids in South America, which I know from reading a great number of books. Jaguars live in South America also. I would like to see a jaguar someday, but probably I will not. In the painting, a person stood on the top of the pyramid. It looked like a woman, but the figure was very tiny and I am not artistic. She held her arms straight up, toward the moon rising over the pyramid. I could not help but think of the mirror. I had not been able to find it again once they moved Mrs. H's things into the house. Maybe the moon had gotten out of the mirror and decided to live in my painting instead.

I was a child and when you are a child you think things like that.

Mr. H sent word by telegraph that I was to stay in my rooms so as not to make worry for Mrs. H once they returned. If I liked I might spend my days on the boardwalk once my lessons were done, but at night I must obey Miss Enger, eat what is left over, and look after myself. Surely I had enough toys and books to amuse any girl. Miss Dougall minded me like a pot of boiling water. The housemaid locked my door at night and kept me out of the front rooms with the end of a broom. Miss Dougall was the sheriff of my father's law and every night I wished she would fall down the stairs and bust her big curly head. She did not oblige me. Miss Enger patted my hand in sympathy but did not unlock my door or bring me anything extra to eat.

I sat at my window. I spun the chamber on Rose Red and ran my fingers over the pearls in the grip. There were a lot of them by then. I had pleased Mr. H often, but it had been a good bit since he'd given me any new pearls. If I obeyed Miss Dougall perhaps I would get another. This idea cheered me up some.

Things began to happen all in a row: I knew my father and Mrs. H had come home, I could hear them laughing and walking and banging forks against plates. But I was not called for. My food was brought. My linens seen to. Miss Enger did not come to see me anymore. Mrs. H sent her on her way with a fair clutch of money and a reference. A new Irish hall girl drew the chore of my lessons. She was called Moira Daly and could not herself read. She was very apologetic, however, and I took it on myself to teach her letters so that somebody between the two of us could learn a thing. Still, no one called for me. Miss Daly was not nearly brave enough to take my questions downstairs.

In the evening, I could hear Mrs. H playing the pianoforte. She was very good at it. She sang as well, and was particularly fond of strange old songs like *Hymn to the Evening Star* and *Fairies of the Hill*. I lay against the floor and listened every night. I drank her voice up like milk.

I had never heard a woman sing before. Only the coyote in his cage and the seagulls crying.

After Miss Daly's lessons each morning, I crept out of my window and shimmied down the olive tree. I came away yellow with olive pollen and ran up to my boardwalk where Thompson the fox waited for his bowl of sarsaparilla. Florimond wandered around his paddock on his hind legs, looking for a trainer to praise him. I gave him the apples from my breakfast. I do not care for apples.

I played cards with Thompson in my saloon. He had lost the trick, but I suspected he had the Queen and I was done for already. Thompson chewed on the seven of spades.

A shadow moved over the saloon-door. It was not a groundskeeper's shadow. It was not a bear's shadow. I looked up and I will confess I was angry. No one was allowed up there but me. Miss Enger, Miss Bornay, even rotten Miss Dougall knew they had no power here. They had the whole house and the world on top. The saloon was my place, and whoever it was would not get any sarsaparilla. But it was not Miss Enger or Miss Bornay or Miss Dougall.

Mrs. H stood in the doorway. She wore a vermillion dress. With the sun behind her she looked like a planet on fire. Her heart-shaped face was blank. I suddenly felt very shabby and small in my playdress. She was ever so much taller and prettier than I would ever be. Wherever they invented women like that, it was country I could never even visit.

Thompson leapt away from the table and skittered under the bar. Mrs. H moved in her greyhound way, her heels clicking on the floorboards. She sat down and took up the red fox's cards, fanned them out like an old gambler. She slotted the seven of spades into her hand, bending back the chewed-up part. Her fingers had nail paint on them which I had never seen before, not being acquainted with many fine women. I stared. The paint looked like blood. Was she sick? She was so pale and her nails so red. Did she hunt, like me, and dress her own kills? Had she killed something today and forgotten to wash herself? Mrs. H said nothing. She drew a card from her hand laid it down between us. I could see the green ring better. It was an uncut emerald the size of a man's knuckle with fiery flaws winking down at the bottom of it like fish in a pond.

Mrs. H laid down the Queen of Spades. I'd lost. The Queen of Spades has black eyes and black hair, like me, but her gown is red, like Mrs. H's.

"So you're the little Indian child," she said, and those were Mrs. H's first words to me. She looked all around the room. Looking at her felt like drinking something harsh and strong. It woke you up and made you dizzy all at once. Her eyes were green like her ring.

"I can see we have a lot of work to do," she sighed.

My whole body felt like I had when I touched the mirror under the muslin. Like a candle melting into icewater.

"Please," I whispered. "Don't be mean to me. I'm good. I promise I'm good." That sounded babyish and nonsensical out of my own mouth. I tried again. I spit in my hand and held it out like I'd seen Mr. H do with horse-breeders. "If you love me, I'll love you back," I bargained.

Mrs. H laughed. The wind picked up outside. I did not think she would shake on it but she did. Her fingers were cool on mine. She avoided my spat-upon palm and wiped her hands on her skirt afterward.

Mrs. H reached over the card table and smoothed my hair between her fingertips. "You are not entirely ugly, but no one would mistake you for a human being. That skin will never come clean. And that hair! Black as coal, and those lips, as red as the hearts your savage mother no doubt ate with relish. That's all right. All women have a taste for hearts. But you will discover that I am a gentle soul. If you do as I say and imitate me as best you are able, perhaps you will find yourself gentled as well. It is not beyond possibility that God will overlook your coarser half and take you to His bosom at the end of days."

Mrs. H stood up. Her dress rustled like breath. She walked over to the slot machine and pulled the arm without dropping a coin into its mouth. The reels spun. Four red apples whirled up, glossy and dark. I had spun that beast a thousand times and never seen one apple. Silver dollars exploded into the pan like rifle-fire. Mrs. H left them there. She left the door swinging. She left me alone.

From that day forward she never used my name. Eventually I forgot it. Mrs. H called me something new. She named me cruel and smirking, she named me not for beauty or for cleverness or for sweetness. She named me a thing I could aspire to but never become, the one thing I was not and could never be: Snow White.

PART II

Snow White
Contends with
the Prairie-Falcon's
Blindness

Snow White
Fights a Lump of Pitch

I **do not believe** any person is born knowing how to be human. Everyone has to learn their letters and everyone has to learn how to be alive.

A is for Alligator. B is for Beauty.

Maybe it's not a lesson so much as it's a magic trick. You can make a little girl into anything if you say the right words. Take her apart until all that's left is her red, red heart thumping against the world. Stitch her up again real good. Now, maybe you get a woman. If you're lucky. If that's what you were after. Just as easy to end up with a blackbird or a circus bear or a coyote. Or a parrot, just saying what's said to you, doing what's done to you, copying until it comes so natural that even when you're all alone you keep on cawing *hello pretty bird* at the dark.

When Mrs. H said I was not human she meant I was not white. She was wrong about the reason but not about the thing. I wasn't human. I was a small device who knew only how to shoot a gun, play the slots, and dress up in fancy clothes to please a rich man. Nobody had ever loved me proper and if there's a boring story in this world, that's it. I want to skip this part. I want to pull on the arm of my slot machine and let the rolls flip over until they show a green tree in the summertime, and me away from that house, walking tall under a blue sky. I want to skip this part but I am here to tell you: a stepmother is like a bullet you can't dig out. She fires true and she fires hot and she fires so quick that her metal hits your body before you even know there's a fight on. I didn't even know what white was.

So here's the truth of it: there was blood and some of it came from between my legs and some of it came from my face where Mrs. H struck me over and over, because I was bad, because I looked like my mother, because I smelled like an animal, because I did not show her any human feeling or sweetness and that made me wicked. It is my understanding that when you start bleeding you are a woman so I guess that's what I was.

She put jasper and pearl combs in my hair and yanked them so tight I cried—*there, now you're a lady*, she said, and I did not know if the comb or the tears did it. She put me in her own corsets like nooses strangling my waist til I was sick, my breath gone and my stomach shoved up into my ribs—*there, now you're civilized*, she said, and I did not know if it was the corset or the sickness that did it. She forbade me to eat sweets or any good thing til I got thin as a dog and could hardly stand I was so damn hungry—*there, now you're beautiful*, she said and I did not know if it was my dog-bones showing or my crawling in front of her begging for a miserable apple to stop my belly screaming that made me fair.

For myself I thought: this is how you make a human being. A human being is beautiful and sick. A human being glitters and starves.

I worked hard to be as human as possible.

She dismissed Miss Marie the kitchen maid and Miss Mary the laundry maid. She dismissed Miss Bea the scullery. Mr. H gave up the house to her. He did not bring me a pearl for obeying Miss Dougall. The house was hers to lord over, was the word of Mr. H. Children are the province of women and none of his nevermind now, thank God in heaven.

When she hit me, she said she loved me. When she scratched my face, she said she loved me. And let me tell you, Mrs. H loved me most of all the day she locked me in my room with no lamps or candles because I looked too long at a groomsman and that's the mark of a whore, a slattern with a jackal for a mother, hellion trash with an animal heart. For a week I had no bath or books, no light and no food, but she loved me the whole time, whispering through the door that her love could burn the whore out of me. Love could make me pure again.

On account of all of this I had some peculiar ideas about love. I'll tell you what I thought on the subject back then: it's about as much use as a barrel with no bottom. When I fed the pigs and two of them got to scrapping over an old soft onion, I thought: that's love. Love is eating. Love is a snarling pig snout and long tusks. Love is a dress like the sun. Love is the color of blood. Love is what grown folk do to each other because the law frowns on killing.

I said I loved her back. I put my hand on the door and I said I loved her back and when I said it I thought of kissing her and also of shooting her through the eye.

Mrs. H dismissed Mrs. Whitney the housekeeper and Mrs. Kenny the cook. She dismissed Miss Daly who could write her name by then and did not seem sad to go. The men servants she left, excepting the groomsman I looked at. There were no ladies left but us.

How will we keep the house?

You will keep it. A clean house creates a clean soul and you have work to do. This is what it means to be a woman in the world.

When Mrs. H locked me up in the dark that time, I cobbled up a second notion. Love was a magic fairy spell. Didn't the girls in my books hunt after love like it was a deer with a white tail? Didn't love wake the dead? Didn't that lady love the beast so hard he turned into a good-looking white fellow? That was what love did. It turned you into something else.

For this reason, I forgave Mrs. H. I tried to be near her all the time. She only meant to scrub me up and fix me. At any moment, she might take me in her arms and kiss me and like that beast with a buffalo's body I would fill up with light and be healed. Love would do what it did best. Love would turn me into a white girl. If I did everything right, one day I would wake up and be wise and strong, sure of everything, with skin like snow and eyes as blue as hers. It would happen like a birthday party. One day the girl in the mirror would not look like me at all, but like my stepmother, and nothing would hurt anymore forever.

Snow White
Deals the Dead Man's Hand

I hunted Mrs. H and I hunted her mirror. My father hunted the blue and the yellow down a long mountain range like a wrinkle in the world. I guess we're pretty much alike when you think about it. Only he got clear of that house and it took me quite awhile to fix that for myself.

A house is a kind of box you put a girl in. Mrs. H and me, we rattled around in it like two old bullets. I looked in the basement for her mirror and I was not afraid of the spiders down there. I looked in the attic and I was not bothered by the mice. Mice have their own troubles with cats and whatnot, they do not mind a body. I looked while I cleaned. I looked while I cut up chicken and potatoes. I looked while I boiled linens. I looked in the bedroom of Mr. and Mrs. H and this did fear me something awful, for I would have caught a beating to end them all if Mrs. H found me worrying her things. I sat on their bed, which had red curtains and red pillows and red stairs leading up to it like the bed was a red tower in a white forest. I put my hands into the sleeves of her dresses and that made me shudder. It was like standing inside Mrs. H and wearing her and that is full uncanny, I can tell you. I sat at her lady's table which had a mirror even though it was not the right mirror. This mirror had a frame like a sunburst with little carnelians and opals all over it. I saw myself in it, no more or less than myself: almost fourteen, all long bones, long hair and big black eyes. I did not know to say if I was pretty. I did not look like Mrs. H, so I guessed I was not.

I pulled the silk paper off her lipstick and rubbed it between my fingers. I knew how lipstick got itself made because Mr. H did a fair business selling low-grade garnets. Some fancy men in Paris crush them up into a powder finer than salt and stir the gems in with deer fat. They put a sweet scent on it but I could still smell the deer. When I put it on my lips I could taste it. The blood and the beating of the deer's fright in the forest. I smelled her perfume. It gave me the oddest feeling, like I was smelling an emerald. But not a real emerald, which I imagine has no particular smell. Best I can explain is that stopper was soaked in a smell like the *idea* of an emerald, the idea of greenness and growing and wealth, a kind of fine light that could make a rock bloom.

Mrs. H smelled like jewels. Like the produce of the earth that Mr. H chased all over here and gone. She smelled like a perfect high-yield mine and I got out of that room on the quick.

I found the mirror on account of the paintings in my dime museum. Sometime in the autumn they changed to hunting scenes: Chinese men shooting arrows at an ugly black unicorn, Spaniards hauling harpoons at a giant squid with a whale in its ropy arms, sourfaced men sitting on top of stacks of buffalo like thrones of meat. Thompson the red fox did not like these paintings but I reassured him. I thought of the seagull with my bullet in her eye. I ran my fingers over Rose Red in her holster, the red pearls on her grip. Probably I did not please Mr. H anymore at all. I reckoned Rose Red could not kill a whale or a thousand buffalo but if a stunted black unicorn with an antler for a horn and tiger stripes on its rump got a hankering for red fox, I could handle the situation.

In considering my shootout with the unicorn, I came to see the corner of the painting was curling up away from the frame a little. A Chinese woman with gold ink in her dress covered her eyes so as not to see the skinning of the unicorn nor the sharing out of the liver and the heart, which I have heard hunters do to honor the dead thing, or else perhaps those parts are tasty. I picked at her a little and she gave way like she couldn't wait to get out of the whole scene.

Underneath the weeping lady, Mrs. H's silver mirror peeked out.

I rolled up the painting and rested it on the top of the frame—that familiar wooden frame like cold stone. I hadn't recognized it. I admit that I am a damn fool sometimes. The mirror showed the same black starless sky as before. I looked into it for a long while. The sun in the world outside the mirror turned orange and then red like a leaf in a hurry but inside the mirror it stayed night. I set out my feelings on the matter in an orderly fashion, a poker hand on the table of my spirit.

Pair of Aces: this is my place and she has been here. She has left part of herself here. She has invaded the place where I am most myself and stuck a flag in it. Pair of Eights: this is my place and she has made it hers but that goes both ways. I have this piece of Mrs. H and it belongs to me. She put it in my kingdom.

Queen of Diamonds: she left part of herself here to watch me.

Snow White
Juggles Her Own Eyes

he moon came on in the mirror.

This time I did not run off. The mirror was an animal, like Thompson or the crocodile. You have to show it you're not gonna hurt it, maybe feed it a little, before it stops thinking you're prey or predator or both. I fed the mirror my face and the moon came on inside it like a huge white eye. I had already seen this trick. But I did not know how to make it do anything else. I just kept looking into it, counting craters, and I guess the mirror got fed up because the moon started creaking and spinning and before the dark side came around to the light it had turned into Mrs. H on her knees scrubbing a marble floor with pink veins forking through it.

Mrs. H was young. You could tell she wasn't Mrs. H yet. Her whiskey-colored hair was braided up tight and I could see dirt under her fingernails. She scrubbed and scrubbed and my hands tingled where I had rubbed them raw scrubbing just that morning. Young Mrs. H looked up at a fine lady in a primrose dress and I heard her say something real quiet like the mirror was a muzzle.

Why do I have to work on my knees? We have more maids than books in the library. Mrs. H held out her hands. Lye burns slicked them like shiny snail-tracks.

The woman in the primrose dress answered: *this is what it means to be a woman in the world. Work until you die and work again after. Your only choice is whether you scrub the vaults of hell or the halls of heaven. Anyone who tells you different is a huckster with his hand in your pocket.*

The brush in Mrs. H's hand blinked out and with a quickness she was bent over in the hearth in a yellow apron, picking out hard little peas. Her face was full of ash like a Catholic in spring. The same fine lady wore a cornflower dress.

Why do I have to comb the grate? We have charwomen and sculleries as plentiful as water. Mrs. H held out her hands. Ash turned them dead and grey.

The woman in the cornflower dress answered: *this is what it means to be a woman in the world. Obey until a man gives you permission to die and keep on obeying after. The tasks you're handed make less sense than a rooster in a Sunday hat, but if God wanted us to have a say he'd have made us men.*

The hearth hissed away like steam and young Mrs. H stood in a forest blacker and older than any white pine I'd shot a squirrel out of. She was crying. Up until then I had never seen anyone cry but me, and suspected I was the only one who could do it. I was the only body weak enough. Everyone else had a strong thing inside them where I had tears, and that strong thing protected them against sadness. But young Mrs. H was crying and no mistaking. She unbuttoned her dress and pulled out her laces and stepped naked out of her skirt into the night. The same terrible eyeball of a moon that lived in the mirror shone down and turned her blue. I had never seen a naked woman before. I could not breathe right and my heart ricocheted all over the inside of me like a misfired bullet. Mrs. H looked like a person come to visit from another planet. Her breasts and her belly glowed aquamarine, her muscled legs moved like I imagined that striped, antlered unicorn in the painting moved, graceful as a star coming up in evening. That hair like a long, stiff drink covered her hind parts which made me sorry. I wanted to look at her forever.

Mrs. H dropped to the ground and hit that forest with both fists. She cried and she screamed and she grabbed at the mud, smearing it all over her and scratching herself bloody. *Get me out*, she said into the earth. *Get me out.*

Well, I guess in New England there's things living under the world that answer when you holler at them like that. Two arms bigger than stovepipes came up out of the loam and the grime, and the arms were loam and grime and leaves and roots, and they wrapped around Mrs. H like the tenderest husband ever born. A stony hand stroked her hair I heard a quiet voice like it was a long way off, but so close it whispered right in my ear:

This is what it means to be a woman in this world. Every step is a bargain with pain. Make your black deals in the black wood and decide what you'll trade for power. For the opposite of weakness, which is not strength but hardness. I am a trap, but so is everything. Pick your price. I am a huckster with a hand in your pocket. I am freedom and I will eat your heart.

The loamy arms gathered Mrs. H close in. A still pool opened up under her body like a bloodstain. The water shone clear and perfect as a mirror. For a second she floated on top of the pool, then it flowed around her, up over her skin and into her mouth, filling up all the empty places in her body and pulling her down into the starry slick of it. Under the surface, her face looked so happy. But that's not what I mean. I mean her face *was* happiness. Like her perfume was an emerald. Every time I seen a body take on joy in my life, it's only been a shiver of that blue face in the dark wood, a little piece of her smile or her tears. When the water let Mrs. H go, she came up dry as a prairie, wearing a dress the color of dirt. Green jewels like moss crowded the silk, silver jewels like rivers ran through it, red gems like poison berries wound around her hips and Mrs. H was wearing the forest. She didn't have a speck of mud on her. She had a ring on her finger with a chunk of rough green stone fixed into it.

A distant music picked up and my stepmother moved toward it, starting to dance in time to the mandolins, the lights of some grand ball waltzing already on her skin.

Now, I have had a long time to cogitate on this. I guess I know something about magic after everything that's happened, enough to know you don't go talking about it when it's not around. But I think back east they have Puritan magic and out west we have animal magic and I'll tell you the truth for nothing, those goodies and goodwives and poppets and dark woods scare me worse than any crow with the sun in her mouth.

Snow White
Wears Her Insides on Her Outside

Mrs. H bathed me in milk on Sundays. She poured ice into that milk like sugar and the cream got so cold it burned me like fire. I lay in there trying not to quake or shiver none as Mrs. H called that a weakness. My toes got so you could stick pins in them and I'd never know it. The bathtub was black, from Hungary which is a place I only know the name of. White milk and black stone and me in the middle of it like a cork.

Mrs. H said it would turn my skin white. She said it would wash out my dark parts and better than any soap. Milk had power in the formulation of Mrs. H's mind. Milk comes from creatures that eat only grass and drink only water and do not pollute their bodies with death. Milk comes from mothers. You can see from this that she did teach me things. When she started on this kind of talk my heart toppled over. If she was in a teaching mood she wasn't in a hitting mood. Like sneezing and keeping your eyes open, Mrs. H couldn't do both at once.

Came a night she put me in the milk bath and I thought I'd die of the cold. The hairs on my arms tried to stand up and run off. She dunked me in and shoved my head under the cream and kept it there. I thrashed a good bit but Mrs. H was strong. I couldn't see nothing but white. *Shhhh.* Mrs. H could sound so soft when she wanted. *Shhhh. Let it happen. Take it in. It's inside you, that's the trouble. You don't speak Crow, you don't paint your face. For Heaven's sake, I know more about your mother than you do. It's inside you. Drink it in. What's inside you needs cleaning. Swallow it down and you'll come out pure.*

I choked. I drank it. It went up my nose and I stopped breathing. I hit her across the breast and the chin trying to dig up from that milk that stunk like perfume. The white in my eyes started to go dark and she let me up all the sudden like my skin burned her.

After I squinted real close at the mirror but I didn't look no different.

Snow White
Covers Her Tracks With Her Tail

You may not know it but the keeping of a large house by one girl is the hardest work going on earth. I heard there's fire in hell but I'll bet the Devil just hands you a bucket and tells you to get moving, this place ain't gonna clean itself.

Snow White's Stepmother
Gives Birth to the Sky

I **could not say** exactly how Mrs. H managed to catch pregnant. Mayhap Mr. H fired a baby into her from Peru with a better gun than mine. Probably he came home and performed his husbandry and left again before the sun could surprise him at it.

More to the point, I could not say exactly whether or not Mrs. H *was* pregnant. Her belly did not get bigger nor did she let out her dresses. She said nothing more about it after the announcement which was reported in all the newspapers. I was coming up on seventeen and some noise was made about the necessity of marriage, but Mrs. H did not feel I was fit to entertain suitors and anyway I would not be getting my hands on any of the H money, so there seemed little purpose in it. *I've half a mind to dump her over the border in Crow territory and let them kill her or marry her or whatever those heathens do with beasts less useful than a horse but prettier than a cow.*

Well, at least I knew my worth.

Mrs. H came pretty often to the dime museum. She rolled up the painting of the Chinese unicorn and looked at herself in the mirror. Sometimes she talked to the mirror like it was a person. Sometimes she asked it questions. I never heard it answer but it must have or she wouldn't keep asking. Sometimes she pressed her cheek to her reflection in the glass.

The woman in the mirror was pregnant.

The reflection of Mrs. H got big in the belly day by day as the winter wore on. Mrs. H stayed slim as a pen. She moved her hand over her flat stomach; in the mirror Mrs. H cradled her roundness in both arms. The paintings in the museum changed to Madonnas, women in blue on seashells and star-points and sitting on silver thrones. The parrots died. I found them with frost hardening on their beaks. I said goodbye to them in French but that is all I know how to say so it was a short eulogy. Whenever I looked in the mirror after Mrs. H left, all I saw was the copy of her, humming a song while she let the waists of her dresses out with a quick, clever needle. Once she looked at me, looked out of the mirror and into me. She put her hand on her stomach and whispered: *soon.*

I ran.

The baby came at night. I watched it happen from my hiding place and if I live a hundred years I will not see anything stranger. Mrs. H stood stock still while the reflection in the mirror cried and struggled and bled. The blood coming from between her legs wasn't red. It was the color of a mirror, like mercury beading out of her. She looked like she would die and the baby would choke on her. Drown in her like a dress. Mrs. H just folded her hands in the museum and never made a sound. She watched. She didn't even fidget. Finally the child spilled out of the woman in the mirror, mirror-blood gushing and a rope of that terrible black wood like stone connecting them. The woman in the mirror cut it with her teeth. The child was a boy.

He did not look very much like Mr. H.

But then, neither do I.

Mrs. H laid her hand on the glass. The baby didn't cry. Sticky silver stuff covered his skin. The woman in the mirror put the baby to her breast and the mirror flowed out of her body, overflowing his tiny mouth and trickling down his cheek. The woman in the mirror smiled and knuckled the drop away.

And that was it.

The boy did not come out of the mirror, which was what I expected to happen. Mrs. H came to see him often enough, but he was born in the mirror and looked fit to stay there. I came to visit him, too. I wanted to see my brother. The woman in the mirror tilted him up in her arms so I could get a better look. He got big fast—after a week or two he was walking around in there and running up to the glass when I came in, putting up his hands like he wanted to touch me. He liked me to put both my hands up against his, ten fingers and ten fingers.

I guess he was a nice baby. I don't know much about them. He had small pink fists. He was a healthy white baby who would own the whole world if he could get out of that mirror. The newspapers said Mr. H had a son and heir. But my father never came home to shake his son's little fist and welcome him into the world that had been made to fit him like a good suit. He never came home much at all. I thought to myself that Mr. H was not his father and I was not his sister but that Mrs. H got a baby from the pool in the forest and he came out in the mirror. But I did not like thinking that. The baby smiled when he saw me. That was nice. Nobody did that before.

I wished the mirror would just show the damn moon again. The rest of it put me in a black mood and that's the truth.

Snow White
Wears the Sun

I believe the boy in the mirror was about five when Mr. H sent word he would be arriving home on the Saturday evening train.

Mrs. H said I would have to try to look pretty. She took me into her bedroom and thought that was a big favor on her part, but only because she did not know I had already been in there looking for her mirror. The Mr. Buttons had filled the milk bath already. Ice floated in it. I had got a fair sight older and grown breasts (which I did not ask for) and I did not want to be naked in front of Mrs. H but when I held onto my clothes she got out shears and cut them off of me. I stood there with my arms over myself and laundry scum on the backs of my hands. Mrs. H waited and pretty soon it dawned on me that she couldn't lift me anymore. I got in the milk; it hurt like lye.

Mrs. H screwed up her thoroughness and let it loose all over me. She scrubbed my hair and rubbed that cream into my skin with a boar-hair brush and made me hold ice both my mouth and my womanly parts until it melted. I did not cry but I wanted to. *This is what it means to be a woman in the world. You have to get pure. You have to get clean. You just won't do filthy and indecent and smelling like fox. Do it for your father. You love your father. You want him to be happy.*

Mrs. H dried my hair and combed it out. She put oils into it that I did not enjoy the smell of. My hair was very long then and she wound it around and around like a big black snake, fixed it up on top of my head and put ruby pins through it. Some of them pins pricked my scalp and I felt a little blood trickle down the back of my neck. Mrs. H produced a number of contraptions into which she crammed and pinched my body so that my breasts squished up and my waist tied down tiny like hers. She trembled a little bit. I was not accustomed to seeing her tremble. She seemed mighty upset, maybe even feared, though I wouldn't know fear in that face if I saw it.

Mrs. H pulled a dress out of a steamer trunk and it was the color of the sun. It had a high bustle and sharp pleating at the skirt-hem and a neckline I wanted to run away from. It looked like fire. It looked like molten iron. I didn't want to be inside that dress. It was going to burn me. It was going to eat me. But Mrs. H dug her nails into my arm. *Do this thing and you can call me mama. Do this thing and you can have anything you want.* She dragged it down over my head. It hung so heavy. *Everyone trades their heart for their children, you know.*

"I know you can do magic," I said to her. I said it to hurt her. I said it to make her wear a dress of fire, too. But she wasn't hurt. She never hurt.

Mrs. H stopped strangling me in the stays of that beast. Her heart-shaped face didn't ever show anything to me I could understand. "And what do you think magic is, my little Snow White?"

"I saw in the mirror. What you did in the forest. And how the lady in the mirror had that baby."

Mrs. H stared at me for a long time. I was as tall as she was. We stood there like the same woman except her dress was blue.

"Let me tell you something, kid," said Mrs. H of Boston and Beacon Hill. "Magic is just a word for what's left to the powerless once everyone else has eaten their fill."

Snow White
Compares Herself to An Unmovable Rock

I heard a lot of talk speculating on whether myself or Mrs. H was the more handsome. It's plain foolishness.

Everybody knows no half-breed cowgirl can be as beautiful as a rich white lady. Where's your head at?

PART III

Snow White and Porcupine Chase Each Other Around the World

Snow White
Stops Speaking

This is where Snow White gets off. Where she stops telling a story about other folk and starts being in a story other folk tell. It's like crossing a cold stream. You don't even think much about it—water's not that deep, and only a few miles further on there's a meal and a bed. But you've left one country and hoofed it on into someplace else.

Girl deserves a rest, anyhow. You can tell a true story about your parents if you're a damn sight good at sorting lies like laundry, but no one can tell a true story about themselves.

Snow White
Steals the Sun's Tobacco

Snow **White knows** when it's time to blow the scene. Saddle her whole life and get on the road. It's a sense like smell or seeing, when she looks around at a pretty little zoo and realizes it doesn't belong to her, she belongs to it. Ain't never going to be the hero in this story, kid, way things are headed. Just meat for the table. Best be on your way. Kiss the bear and the fox and don't look back. Spin those slots one last time. Don't they come up all winter, white as death. Don't they always. Don't they just.

So this is what happens: girl gets her gun, puts on a man's clothes, steals a horse, and lights out for Indian Territory.

Snow White's heard her daddy's men talk about Indian Territory. They're skeered and scarred and when they say those words it sounds like their whole world is surrounded by a jungle of cannibal Oberons and night-blooming thunderbirds. Eat you alive and wear your skin, won't they? What roads they got are lined with white men's skulls. If a body gets lost in there he'll never unsee what goes on, painted men dancing and songs like your mother dying and witches boiling bones and girls what turn into wolves. God don't open His eye there. It's Hell or fairyland or both.

Snow White says: sounds good to me.

You've read the papers. That girl run off because she got prettier than her mama and *oh ho* the old lady don't like that! You know how mothers and daughters are. As if a body don't just get fed up. As if a kid don't have a limit on hardship.

So Snow White throws her dress in the furnace to burn like it ought to. She doesn't even wait for sundown. Just hoofs it while Mrs. H gets herself gorgeous. Snow White straps Rose Red to her hip and rides out on a big apron-faced Appaloosa with spots on his rump like eyes. So what if it's stealing? She took her daddy's hat, too. Snow White can ride so sweet you'd think there's no horse under her, just a girl with four legs pounding the ground. Fuck that mirror and fuck that house. What's she owe them? Her back, that's what. The girl is gone. She is plum finished. She walks out through the front door. It's night and everything smells like the sea.

Snow White points her situation north, toward the queen hanging upside down in the sky, punished forever for using her daughter poorly. That's the road for her, yes sir, toward Montana, toward the future, out of the world and into the black.

Snow White
Dances With Porcupine

Not too long before somebody picks up her trail. He has a name but it doesn't matter. He has a job. That's who he is. He's a Pinkerton, but that doesn't matter either. Who isn't, these days? If you've got a gun arm on you, that is. If you've got a proclivity for hitting people until they do as they're told. This dude, he come out from Chicago with a job in his holster. Don't care who hired him; don't care how long it takes. He gets his money every week by wire and that's as good as being on the right side of virtue in his book.

It's not the hardest job he's ever done. Girl don't really know where she's going, see. It's a long way to Montana. What she knows about long-haul travel she read in books and the man's read those books, too. These runaways, they're easy money. Wastrel trigger-punks with less sense than Dog gave a gopher. (This is how the dude appellates the good Lord for he does not abide blasphemy. The Great Good

Dog in Heaven watch over your humble servant.) Those abandons are nothing but walking sacks of coin to him. They shin out like the world's got room for them but it just ain't so. Boys end up shot in some Babylon of a gold town. Girls go to ruin. This gives the dude a grand ticket to visit any brothel he passes, and the dude do like roostering himself up a spell. Once he's got a bead on her. Once he smells her good and full. He got a late start, is all. Train from out east don't make the trip in a blink. Pretty soon she'll bake that crowbait horse into the ground and he'll have her. Once she's riding shank's mare she'll be easy as nickels.

The conditions of the job don't bother him none. He's done worse. Most runaway jobs don't necessitate his gun or his knife, but it's a bad old country out there these days. Folk want all sorts of loot for their trouble. The dude's had to bring back ears, hair, fingers, even an union-man's eyeball once. The eye was bright blue. Easier than hauling the whole body over three states, he'll tell you that much for free. Sometimes he thinks the rich are so different from usual folk they're more like wild beasts or fairies than men. If this fellow had a gentle stomach he'd have taken up some other business. He does everything a Marshal does but twice as hard, twice as dirty, and without the soft and cushioning arms of the government to wipe his tears.

The dude don't see himself as a bad man. Way he sees it, he's an angel for hire. He can gather in lost lambs from the four corners and kiss away their tears or he can shake a flaming sword. Up to his employers. St. Michael don't question why when the Big Dog says git. Ole Mike, he just ties up his war-bag, thumps his golden road, eats his beans out the tin and when he sees his mark he gets to it no fuss. That's the dude in a nut. There's nights he don't feel so fine on it, sure enough. But nobody likes their job sun out and sun in. Reckon there's bankers back east right sick of the smell of money. Reckon they might like a change. But there comes a time when a man is who he is and not even a railroad spike through the chin can change it. That banker will be counting coin in his grave and come the great good day when righteous folk put on their white robes, the dude will still be a Pinkerton with an eye on his chest, minding Heaven don't go apples up.

No, the dude don't call himself a bad man.

But he's got bad business to tend to.

Snow White
Shoots Antelope By Means of a Magic Arrow

Snow **White's pony** bears up just fine. She never could abide the trussed-up old world high-steppers Mrs. H favored. Pintos, paints, and appies, accept no substitutes. Snow White helped the birth of this horse in particular. Shoveling horse shit and afterbirth beat laundering a household full of button trousers seven ways. Hell is a soapcake on Monday morning. She'd cleaned the blood out of his eyes and the muck out of his tail. Old boy has a pedigree name in a ledger somewhere, but Snow White's called him Charming ever since he mashed her foot flat half a minute after he came into the world trying to tottle up to standing.

Snow White rides him hard, no mistaking. She needs distance, the generosity of miles. Maybe there's no gone that's far enough, but if there is, she aims to find it. She lets

Charming snatch up sea-grass and when the sea's so far behind them she can't smell salt, she directs him to alfalfa and meadowsweet. Snow White portions out a bag of apples she absconded with between herself and her horse. She still does not care for apples but food is food. Sugar is sugar. She has to make them last. All the smarts in the world don't tell you where the next town lies when you've never seen the big open but in pictures. Don't matter much. She's never been happy a day in her life until she lit out hell for Hades, and if she never sees another human face it's just as well by her. Snow White puts her gun on her arm and takes down a beaver for a week's suppers. She's not too sure how to dry it perfect, but she does her best, and the fur sits better on her shoulders than any dress she ever wore to please her daddy. She's careful with her bullets. Gotta miser them good. Her life is weighted out in apples and bullets.

Snow White follows the sun.

This is her father's country. Every town Snow White lights on is a camp with *H* stamped on the gold pans. She keeps her hat down. Waters Charming and rubs him down good. They're muddy, chawed-up shanties with more drink than nuggets. The camps recall to her some mixed-up boot-black funhouse mirror of her boardwalk back home and she understands for the first time what it means to be a rich man's daughter. Even a secret one. Even one worked like a furnace. Snow White drinks whiskey now and it tastes like dirt on fire but it makes her feel strong. She eats son of a bitch stew and before too long she gets to like it: boiled up baby cow brains, liver, tongue, heart, kidneys and on good days a carrot. It stinks powerfully, but her body wants it awful, the blood and the iron and the fat.

Snow White does not know much about men and she does not like what she sees. Their eyes dog her something dreadful. They are for the most part a miserable sight at cards. When Snow White plays, the Queen of Spades always turns up in her hand. She don't like it. Don't like being watched. Oftener than not, some poor overworked girl does all the work of entertaining—tinkles the piano if they got one, serves table, changes the day's chiseling for currency, and there's a menu behind the bar if you got a hunger dinner don't touch. The miners use that girl awful in every place Snow White slows down long enough to scowl. It sticks in her jaw every time. That lady put on a purple skirt and shined herself up and damn but she can play those cowboy songs like she was born on a drive, but they don't see it. Don't see the mighty pains she took on their sorry behalf. Don't see what it *costs* to get so fair.

Snow White can't quite call whether it's her tits or her gun that grief her most. Sure, the grimy boys grab her even when she bands her chest down tight, but once she punches one of them plum down, she gets to like that, too. Turns out her shit-shoveling arm can clean a man's plow no problem. But no matter how she pulls her slicker over Rose Red, some ganted grubstake whose claim don't love him sees the grip and thinks he can take it easy.

Probably it was always going to turn out like it did. Human nature only got a few tales to tell.

In a silver camp name of Haul-Off, Snow White shot a man.

It was raining fierce and the fella hadn't eaten in three days. Any color he struck went eighty percent to the company and how can a man get ahead on those numbers? How can a man think straight with a gun like that in his sight, all those pearls and that opal glinting like a good life?

There's a heap of world Snow White doesn't understand. She can ride and she can shoot and she can hold her rye, she don't fare well in high company and she don't know a thing about cattle. But getting beat down by a body twice your size who just wants to take the one thing you've got in this world from you—yeah. Snow White knows something about that. And she's about the fastest draw til you hit the Dakotas. She did it out in the street out of respect to the piano girl. It feared her less than she thought. No different than a tin goose in a gallery, only she got no prize for firing true. Snow White felt a damn sight worse over the seagull she brought down way back. Funny how a gun can speak your pain so clear.

When she sheaths her barrel, she sees it: one of the red pearls fell off somewhere in the mud. Nobody's daddy is pleased.

Ten miles out of town Snow White broke up sobbing into her pony's mane. Charming stood bold, took all her tears so she could keep on going.

Snow White follows the moon.

Snow White
In the Underworld

Round about Nevada the grass gets scarce and the critters get shy. All those apples are long gone and the bullet situation is not promising. Snow White hitches up her need and goes looking for work. She suffers some worry over whether her femaleness will trouble her, but the truth is after riding those back countries down, most everyone looks the same.

She finds what she's looking for in a gemstone mine south of Blue Coffin. You could ride right over it and never know it's there: the men live below snakes in the hollows left after the axes and drills have stripped the shine out of the rock. Coupla the boys even throw down rugs, perch a picture of the missus back home up on a spit of stone. One hollow's set up for a saloon, a tilted splintery bar, whiskey so cheap and stiff the boys call it Who-Shot-John, a card table and seven stools nobody stops fighting over. Snow White stows Charming with the camp horses in a corral run by a woman just about as old as the wheel and heads underground. It don't escape her this is her father's mine. Nevada is his mother's teat; where he made his fortune. Well, why shouldn't Snow White have a fortune, too? Not that she expects one. She's no fool and a night in a gold camp will straighten you right out on the odds of making your dimes on the lode. If you want to get straight, which most nobody does once they've seen the good blue and the hard yellow.

It's neither of the two down here. It's the true red: rubies. Bloody knuckles; apple rinds. Snow White gets a skinnier cut on account of her being a girl and a half-breed heathen if ever the foreman did see one, but it's something. It keeps Charming in hay and her in beans-on-griddlebread and on Sunday they get tinned peaches if the take's been good. Way Snow White figures it, in a month she'll have enough socked away to head back north, up to Montana which she has not forgotten, into the Territory. In a month she'll have enough to quit worrying if she hasn't seen so much as a badger stumble past her sights. The company man smiles and rolls his cigarette. It's what they all say. *Just a month and I'll bring my people out. Just a month and I'll move up top to Blue Coffin where they got proper houses. Just a month and I'll be shitting rubies, that's how rich I'll strike.* Opium ain't got nothing on the promise of tomorrow turning up better than today.

Snow White does not complain. She swings her ax and learns to see in the dark. She forgets what it's like to smell nice. She gets so that her heart beats faster whenever she sees a glitter of red in the gloom. Just about every week some idiot tries to get her to wash their clothes or scrub them down or show that cook how to make a proper tuck-in. Just about every week some bruiser gets tied and bellows at her to show them her Injun witchcraft or tries to get their hands under her shirt. *Give us a smile, Snowy. Give us a taste. We all share down here.*

Snow White has broken a fair number of fingers. Fingers count in this line of work. Fingers are a penny-bid on your future. All that separates a man from a dog is fingers.

Folk stop galling her so hard. Snow White is aware that if she loses one fight it's over for her. So she does not lose. She cuts her hair off after a short, burly mister starts touching it and allowing as how he's heard heathen's pussy's got feathers instead of hair. *I know y'all are just like a blackbird down there.* She doesn't miss it. No mirrors underground, and she's grateful for that. She swings her ax and does not see the sun. It is like being inside the heart of her father. Close and dark and hungry, pumping wealth like blood.

A month is not enough. Never is and she knows that now. Hell is a company town. Snow White owes the store for the food in her belly, the tools on her back, Who-Shot-John whizzing around her head every night when the all-stop blows. And she might have stayed, told herself the big lie, that tomorrow she'd find a bloody knuckle so big it'd pay her way to the moon with cash to spare. There's an apple in that mountain with her name on it.

But somebody's looking for her. Someone's knocking on the grass up there, and he wants to come in.

Snow White
Gets Hit On the Head With a Brick

All **right, all** right. If you stand her a swallow of Who-Shot-John, the girl will fess up.

Snow White lost one fight. Just one, but it was a fuss to be remembered.

The man in question was a no-account out of Laramie. He'd been a cattleman before a flood took his flock and all his hopes came a-cropper. He'd seen his brother exalted for rustling and his wife dead of the lunger the winter after. It cripples a man in the morality to spend his days digging beauty out of dead rock for the pleasure of rich folk he'll never meet, and this fella was right torqued up. Not that he'd been a stand-up aforehand. He wanted to punch down the hangman who took his kin and the angels who took his girl but they were not present. Snow White, contrariwise, had broken the fingers of a number of his friends and had to sleep sometime. A helpless man swings wide.

So this man followed Snow White back to her hollow with a determination for trouble hanging on his hips. He had once allowed to the boys that she was pretty enough for a godless mix-blood bitch. He'd never ridden Injun, but he'd never et dog before, neither. The world of experience is a broad and unpredictable country. The way the cattleman heard it told, squaws got wolf's fur on their tits and a tail fit for a lizard tucked twixt their flanks. Snow White being only half-squaw he'd likely have to settle for one or t'other but you can't have everything. He'd considered it a long while and figured God owed him some pleasure in this life and if she didn't like it, well, a good pound-down puts anyone in an amenable mood.

Snow White lay asleep. Without thinking about it the cattleman took off his hat when he came into the hollow like he meant to call her ma'm and present flowers. She was awful nice-looking when she was asleep. No scowling or hissing or cursing. Why, if you squinted, she almost looked regular, like some rancher's daughter who just needed a bath and she'd be respectable as a wedding. If she hadn'tve hacked her hair off he'd have judged her the second or third handsomest girl he'd had acquaintance of, and he'd been to Denver once. The cattleman felt a powerful need to kiss Snow White. Mayhap she liked being kissed. Mayhap she'd wake up and show her wolf-parts. In the storybooks, if you woke a girl up with a kiss she belonged to you. It was like a brand on a cow's rump. A kiss round and black and permanent-like on the skin, telling the whole world who owned her. The idea of that big burning kiss made him hard enough to drill rubies.

The cattleman kneeled down and put out his lantern. He kissed Snow White real nice, like you kiss a lady. Her fist cocked his jaw good, but the cattleman had the upper position and she could not reach her gun. He slapped her open hand and yanked on her sawed-off hair.

"I weren't gonna hurt you none," he hissed in the dark, even though he would have if she hadn't looked so damned daisy lying there. He'd kissed her just as sweet as his own wife but it weren't enough for her, no sir. He popped her nose and that felt good. Blood sprayed on her mouth. Blood on her skin. Blood on the ground. Him sitting on her and watching her bleed. That felt good, too. Pretty soon she'd cry and that'd be just cherry.

Snow White got her thumb into the cattleman's eye and he grunted, grabbed her fingers, fixing to break them to show this cow how it felt, but she rolled him off her onto the floor of the hollow. It was dark and she slugged him hard. He hit her back. They clenched up, fisting and gouging in the dark. The cattleman did not like it. The whiskey in his blood had been surging for a fight with a woman, and a fight with a woman ends in her crying and shaking and a fella hushing her all over. Her dress torn and a bit of tit peeking out and quivering. Simple, righteous pleasures. But Snow White just bit him and pounded him and it was no better than fighting a dude in a barrel-house. Just ugly and bruising and the main thing was not to let anyone get to a gun or else it'd be over on the quick. She didn't even put up her hands to defend herself. She didn't even care if he cut her face. Must be the wolf in her, or the lizard.

Snow White took her licks. Nothing she hadn't done before. Bones creaking and wet blood on her hands, the dark all round and no one coming to help her. Point of fact, that was Snow White's home country. That bloody punishing ground in the dark was real familiar. At least this time she hit back. At least this time she got hers. When you've been hit as often as she has, you don't hardly feel it. You go to another place in your head until it's over. Make yourself small and send the part of you that still feels anything to some tiny corner to wait it out. A corner full of tin ducks and red foxes and old bears, where the slots spin up summer every time. It's just a body. Snow White doesn't care about her body. A body is just a tool you use for walking around. Make sure it holds together and whatever else someone does to it matters less than spitting.

The cattleman had his fill of Snow White. He staggered out of her hollow looking like hamburger. Never did find out if she had a tail. Wasn't worth it. When an animal don't even care if it lives or dies, kicking it holds all the fun of kicking a rock.

Snow White
Plays a Trick on Porcupine

The dude is flummoxed. It'll pass.

Easiest track he ever laid his nose to, that's the Dog's honest truth. This girl is not sly. She does not know how to come to town and leave it so quiet the hooch-man don't even remember how his bottle got so low. She does not know how to go so soft and fast her name never hits the ground. That's okay. The dude knows. That kid has punched out some curly wolf in every shithole from home to the high country. Not a single town left unpunched. She even beefed that short-horn back in Haul-Off—right through the eyes, too. Lucky shot. Every soul gets one. The dude is not troubled by his little angelica blowing smoke through a man. Good for her.

But the trail goes cold as a fish in January on the Nevada side of the Sierra range and the dude cannot re-acquire it. Either she's had her temper surgeried on or been ascended bodily to heaven and he'll be damned if he can say which.

Nobody's seen a girl with a ridiculous gun and a powerful eagerness to fight. Nobody's got whisker or whisper of her. He'd been close enough to cut for sign—the hairs of her pony's tail, the shed fuzz of her angoras, the shells of her parlor pistol. But nothing. The whole world clean of her. Now the dude's got nothing but his dick in his hands. Chicago office is not happy. Who's happy in this world? Maybe a mountain cat with a bead on an open sheep-pen. That's about it.

The dude is disappointed but his patience is vast. He has not been euchered, no sir. He just revises his notions on the girl. Most rich babies would have brotheled up or bucked out by now, but not her. She's game. She's in it for real play. She is heeled and she is sour as a new grape. It's a different situation, that's all. His employer did not give him the whole hoyle.

When the dude was a boy his mother told him a story about a girl in a red dress that blew town, humping through the high country on foot. Even back then the dude thought that girl was done crazy. *Somebody better help her, mama, or she's gonna get et. Somebody's gotta track her down and get her back home to her daddy.* Well, sure enough this big old wolf pricks her up and starts after, and he's got a shine on this girl more like a man's than a wolf's. It don't go well in the end—girls and wolfs, they got nothing to talk about. But the dude felt a kinship with that wolf. A profundity, even. That wolf would follow red-dress all the way around the world once he got her in his nose. You could admire that. You could aspire.

And when the dude asks the Great Dog in Heaven to show him the way, it's the wolf he's thinking of. Like God's this powerful big cay-ote up there and the world's his bone. In chapel with his mama he tries to think of a man up on a cross but it just don't fix. No, it's the tricky-clever lolly-tongued red-loving Dog for the dude, amen and all's well.

The dude prays on it a spell.

It comes up in his head like a bubble in a lake. When a dog's hurting, when a dog's hounded and hard-up, what's he do?

A dog goes to ground.

Snow White
Cheats At Cards

Snow **White comes** out of the earth. She blinks a lot; her eyes forgot how to suck up so much light. She don't present much of a woman anymore: filthy with sweat-grime and ruby-dust, white scar on her cheek like a star, clothes hard done by and none too ladylike to begin with, being goatskins, buck trousers, linen shirt, a fish-slicker coat and her daddy's hat like a creased-up crown. Her hair did grow out some. The sun hits her and Snow White feels like her whole body is baking up sweet and good, like she'd never been born before and is trying alive on for the first time. Charming sees her in the corral and starts hopping fit to stampede the mares, calling out her name in his horsey patois.

The dude is waiting for her. Once he had the picture of it, weren't no work in figuring which softheart company daddy would let a woman dig shine. Weren't no sport in it. Easy as sleeping. Nevada is good to the dude, always has been. He's itchy, waiting on her to pop up mole-like from the grass. He's thought about just popping her on the head with the butt of his hog-leg gun, but he figures he deserves himself the treat of a sit-down with this calico. She's given him a good run, best he's had since the war, and that earns her a few more hours in her mortal coil. Besides, she's been down underground so long. It's a right human deed to let her look on the sun awhile before he sends her there on the permanent.

He squares Snow White's debts to the company man. It's no skin off him. The dude is flush and he'll be full fine when he hands over his proofs back in California. The abandon does not like it; she's cagey and looking to bolt but no man on this earth ever declined to have his accounts cleared and she won't neither. She asks his name; he won't give over. Gets her horse geared and the dude enjoys letting her think of him as a black-chapped angel sent by the Dog to secure her. That's just what he is.

"Where you off to in such a lather?" the dude says. "Get yourself niced up a bit. I bet you haven't had soap on you in a bear's age."

The dude feels right fatherly. Takes her down to the crick to wash the underground off of her. Just can't bring himself to shoot her while she's filthy and starving. There's time. Offers her a cake of French-milled soap he brought all the way out from Chicago. Smells like gardenias if you know your flowers, and the dude does. Snow White knows something's skewed but she grabs it, strips off like it's nothing and climbs in the water. She don't shiver even though that stream has to be as cold as a wagon tire. The miner's crud comes off her in black ribbons. The dude watches another girl come out of the blind mole-skin she was walking around in. This one has muscles like a mountain cat and a kind of pretty he doesn't know what to do with. For fairness he'd take her stepmother six days and twice on Sunday. The beauty Snow White's got has nothing to do with him. She's scarred up and suspicious and shameless. Her pretty's not for him. It's like saying the moon's got a fine figure on her. Maybe true, but what good is that to a man?

Snow White puts her men-clothes back on and makes to get on her spotted horse.

"Where you off to in such a lather?" the dude says. He's got a smile that'd knock down the Queen of England when he wants it. "Set a bit and eat, I bet you had nothing but brown beans and pig's assholes down there."

Right there on the grass the dude lays out a nice spread like she can't refuse. She can't. Like most things, it looks like a choice but it's not. He is being magnanimous and it feels good. In Blue Coffin he bought them a lunch fit for a boss: soft rolls, pemmican, applejack, some real tomatoes and mushrooms and a couple of red and white apples just as firm as fists. A bottle of spruce beer with the bubbles still hard. Snow White knows something's warped but it's real food, the kind that's seen sunlight. She eats and watching her eat feels good. The way she shakes when she does it. The way she takes such a big bite of that apple it almost sticks in her throat. The way she chugs down that jack like a man.

"Why'd you run off from your mama?" the dude says real gentle. Snow White looks at him over the core of her apple. She knows the score and the score is not in her favor.

"Ain't your business," she says back.

"Let's pretend it is."

"We can pretend that crick is the fountain of youth, won't make it any more your nevermind what goes between me and my mama."

And Snow White gets up to go. Puts her hand on her cannon and backs off from the dude like it's a choice she can make. But it's too late for that. He's chased her over hell and gone and she's et his food and he's going to do his job. Dog on High knows his soul and his soul is the job and the job will be done on earth as it is in heaven.

"Where you off to in such a lather?" the dude says again. He's got a voice to charm tigers when he wants to use it. "I got a deal for you if you stow that smokewagon and act civilized. I can shoot you faster than you can draw so don't you twitch."

"Says you."

The dude just laughs. The day a dandy's daughter can outshoot a Pinkerton is the day the Good Dog lays down his bone.

"Pull in your horns and sit down, kid," he snaps, and Snow White does it, instantly, unquestioningly. Her bones obey before her brain can buck. It's a voice the dude likes to use on runaways. Daddy's voice and daddy is not happy. Do what you're told. Don't argue with your betters. Somebody learned that girl good.

"Now," the dude says, "I'm gonna shoot you either way. I been contracted for it, I signed for the job, what's gonna happen was always gonna happen and that's above my bend. I am sorry on it, but we all got a bag of nails to carry."

"Then if it's all the same I'd rather not talk it to death. If you work for Mrs. H I'll allow you some pity; but you signed up for what you'll get. She'll thank you with a knife in the eye. We're both walking dead."

The dude hesitates. "She beat you, I suppose?"

Snow White just laughs. The dude feels that laugh in his spine. It saws there on the hard, old bone.

He takes out a deck of cards. The sun prickles the backs. "Well, you and me, girl, we're gonna draw cuts. Aces high. If I pull the high card I'll shoot you where you sit and carve out your heart to bring back to your mama. I will not enjoy that part of this business but it is firmly stated in the terms of my commission. No accounting for rich folks' morals—but I thank you for the warning on the matter of your mother and I will hew to it. If you draw the high card, we'll walk off paces like gentlemen and you'll have a mean chance at walking off clean."

"How do I know you have not got a cold deck?" Snow White asks.

"If you want the shuffle of it, you may have it."

Snow White looks over the cards real careful. The dude does not cheat. He does not have to. He knows he will get his whether he draws a two of diamonds or the King of Diamonds. It looks like a choice but it isn't. Snow White shuffles; the cards spill from one hand to another like a red waterfall. For a minute she looks like a statue of Temperance or Justice, pouring red water between two cups.

Snow White cuts first. Takes her card and holds it. Passes the dude the deck to cut himself, nice and fair. He takes his and without agreeing upon it they turn over at the same time.

The dude lays down the King of Clubs. He smiles.

Snow White holds the Ace of Hearts.

Snow White
and Porcupine Contend for a Buffalo

now White and the dude pace it off. The sky is bright and hot as the beginning of something. Of course she cheated. Don't be silly. Snow White spent half her growing years shuffling cards for no one. She can cut false and she can cut true but she wasn't going to lose when it counted.

They stand in the green grass. Beneath them men are cutting apple rinds out of the dark and will be forever. Snow White's got the sun behind her. It gives her golden ears like a doggy seraphim.

A crack and a whistle. Another one, almost on top of it, like an echo.

Wind picks up and it smells like rain.

What
Snow White
Said to Porcupine
to Bring Him
Out of His Hole

orry about your knee, mister.

And your shoulder, too.

Remember that, if you're cogitating on coming after me again. I can shoot twice before you shoot once.

Also I will always draw the high ace.

I got no soreness on you, mister.

You wait here. There's good black-tail in these mountains and I aim to help you even if you can't see the help in it yet.

You're gonna take a heart back to Mrs. H. A deer's heart, which is the best I can do.

There is more blood in a deer than seems creditable.

Mrs. H is not my mother and you should not name her that. She is a witch.

I do not know what witches want with hearts but it cannot be anything nice.

Take this heart and put it in a wooden box.

Give the box to Mr. George Button who is the valet and abscond yourself if you aim to keep living.

Forget your bounty. Take what you have already got and call it the bettermost part of luck.

Mrs. H is dreadful clever and will probably not be fooled. That is why you cannot get your scratch.

You will have to run away from her. Like me.

One thing I have learned about running away is that once you start there is no end to it.

I know you will have a hard sentiment about having your plow cleaned by a girl but if you think about it I am being as kind as anybody ever is.

If you get yourself back to the corral you can rustle up a sawbones from the boss-man and get yourself patched.

I am going to take your gun and your knife.

That's about all I can do for you.

Snow White
Races Herself

Snow **White hits** the mountains with Charming underneath her, the dude behind her, a hot hurry on either side and a week's wages in her pockets. A new knife strapped to her leg. A new gun on her back. She's running again. Snow White never stops running. Her hands are still red. Blood don't come off real easy. A space opens up between the shootout and Snow White.

It looked like a choice but it wasn't.

Snow White burns the wind.

PART IV

Snow White Lives
With Forty Dragons

Snow White
Hits the Road

Snow **White does** not know it when she crosses over into the Crow Nation. It looks just like the country which is not the Crow Nation. Trees, river, rocks, clouds hunkering down low like they're just as fugitive as she is. It is spring in both Crow Nation and not-Crow Nation. Puff blossoms on the bough and big tulip buds coming up like candles. Deer have velvet on their antlers in both Crow Nation and not-Crow Nation.

Charming drinks from the swollen freshets. He finds the grass here choice. He is happy to be with Snow White again, happy to be running fast again, happy to prowl it over again with his favorite girl.

Snow White comes over a country possessing many cliffs and high stones. A lot of blackberries here, and sap flowing from the trees like whiskey. She does not apprehend the geography, being dog-tired and shot up in the heart even if her skin's still holding together. Snow White don't know it but on the lee side of those blue rocks there's a soft valley full of people. If she turned east a bit she'd clap eye on a village, buckskin huts, fires and a mess of horses. The people there look like her, but not like her. They wear two braids and high pompadours dyed and stiffened. It's not her mother's village—the Crow Nation is still something to see, and it so happens only one old fella with a black scar right through both his lips remembers a cousin's sister's bad-luck daughter by the name of Gun That Sings. But that's one more than Snow White's got in the way of folk fit to speak to who know her mama lived or died.

If she rides down into the valley, this is what will happen: a little girl will see Snow White and start up crying. Snow White will not mean to fear. She'll get off her horse but the girl only cries harder and runs for her father. Other folk will know her now. They'll look at her and they won't smile. They won't see her mother's face on her and welcome her home. Snow White will try to speak but they do not have English nor want the burden of her handling. Her appearance will not comfort. They will not know her for one of them just by looking. Anyway, Snow White presents a figure like a barrow-tramp and she's still wearing blood, some from the dude and some from the deer.

She won't know it, but the little girl whose name is Cold All the Time will say to her father:

I don't want to go with the white lady, Papa. Make her go away. I want to stay here. Why can't we stay here?

A tall man called Busy Horse will sing up with English in his pockets. He'll turn her back.

Go on your way. A white girl alone will only cause us grief. Someone will come looking for you and the price of you will be sky high. One white person is like one steelhead. Once you see the first one, the others are already coming. Go back to Brother

John the American Man and eat a lot of good things. Do not speak to him about us. We keep to ourselves. We do not want white problems. White girls are bad luck.

And that will just about be the end of Snow White. Once you take away the end in sight, not much left to do but pull up the ground over your head. Sometimes the next no is the last one you can take.

If she turns west, Snow White will find something else, half again as strange. There's a town out there, in the un-land between the dirt America's bought and spat on and the territory they haven't got around to snatching yet. Town goes by the appellation of Oh-Be-Joyful. Fitted out with run-off catalogue women, whores, cattle Kates, bandits, desert rats, and gunslingers. All women; all sour on the whole idea of going back where they came from. No law there, but no mercy neither. Do for outsiders all you please, but never for Joyfolk.

Somebody there remembers Gun That Sings, too. She's about as old as the ocean, but she'll talk you dead for free.

Come on, girl. Pick one. Ain't no guarantee of peace either way, but turn that 'loosa's nose toward something other than nothing at all or this time next year you'll be freezing to death on the Arctic Circle with the ghosts of those boys who thought there was a passage straight through this country top to bottom. Those pompadours have no use for a runaway who'll bring down the whole white world on them, and Joyfolk don't give God the time of day. Pick a path and hit the briars.

Snow White veers west.

The setting sun hits her head like a bullet. Gold spills out, spraying the stones and the grass.

Snow White
and the Birds
from Heaven

These are the seven outlaws who run the town of Oh-Be-Joyful in the Montana Territory:

Bang-Up Jackson, cattle rustler with a face like a hoofprint, dead shot, boss lady with hounds at her feet and the sun at her back. Never had no use for a husband after the one who drug her west got himself shot over a cooking pot in Laramie.

Little Mab Volsky, bank robber, bandit queen, pretty as a spring lamb and twice as likely to kick your face in. Did a job at Billings Bank and Trust to the tune of a dandy fortune, and some train in Arizona plum full of horses and silver and oranges. She and her gang ate that gold for days. Took the horses and coin north. Still a few bottles of orange moonshine in Little Mab's cellar. Still a lot of horses in town with an Arizona brand on their rumps.

Cocklebur Macaluso, best wildcat on the Lode, five fat dollars just to kiss her, and not a man ever called himself cheated.

Girl can cock a gun by squeezing her legs together. You know her by her green bustle and her big ruby mouth, you know her by her laugh and the shine of her knife—and you know her by the jags on her face where a broke down cattleman cut her up good because he wanted power over something.

Woman Without a Name, horse thief, run off from the Crow Nation when her family went down red under gun. Her pompadour's slicked up high and stiff and her hand on a mare's head's as sure and cool as rain. She'll ride down a deer until its heart pops and have it skinned and trussed before it knows it's dead.

Old Epharim, bear of a woman, grey in the braid with half a beard coming in. Used to wrestle cougars for a dollar a match in some traveling show. If you can find blank skin between her scars you're a better eye than most. Middle of town sits a big black pan as wide as a bull's back, and the old girl fries up every night whatever she's shot, wrestled, trampled, or scared dead. Shares it out fair-like. Smokes the whole time like a burning beast.

Witch Hex Watson, scamped out of Maine when the snow-hump knocked the cattle down and all the pretty wives called witchcraft on Missus Watson. Girl don't care. Just as well for a one who never liked the stink of cows, never had a hanker for marrying, never had a smile for anyone but scowls enough to go round. And maybe she did know a thing or two, maybe she'd highed to the woods with her skirts up and maybe the old Puritan cold dark boocraft hopped in her pocket like a frog o' green.

Astolaine Bombast, catalogue woman, ordered up like a rare steak, *plees make shore she is pritty and a whyt gurl if you have enny*. Well, she's pritty enough for homesteading but takes no ribbons at the fair. After three dead babies that fellow wanted his money back, pack her up in a box and ship her east to the wife factory. Astolaine lit off before the new model could hit the doorstep, skinning rabbits and scooping mushrooms like her daddy taught her until she walked out of the woods and into a town full of banshees with no love for anyone's history.

Your past's a private matter, sweetheart. You just keep it locked up in a box where it can't hurt anyone.

Snow White
Meets the Red Ants

Her heart's balled up in her chest and she wants to be quit of it, just cut it out and leave it on the road. Shoulda let the dude have it. In the end she can't hardly see no difference atwixt her and that deer she shot down. No use but meat. Charming carries her through a black oak forest and a mess of plum and peach trees and she don't even stop to get that fruit. Snow White don't care. Her body's all her trouble and she won't feed it any sweet thing. That girl's frown sinks so black she don't see them coming til they're on her.

Seven of them bolt riding down a rill in a spring rainstorm, a bunch of Kates dressed afright and hollering. They've got on deerskins and skunk skins and spotted cat skins, pink silk and purple and blue and green, black lace and harlot's satin, cavalry coats with gold braid and tuxedo trousers, widow's veils and stovepipe hats and one had a whole horse skull on her head like a helmet. Another has a belt of cattle horns. The biggest toad in the puddle has a silver breastplate strapped on and lord knows where she got it, robbing a museum train or playing Hamlet on some black-bellied stage in hell. A bunch of bushwhack Titanias looking blue at her and Snow White reaches for her gun. If they're fix to knock her down, she'll welcome it.

That's not what happens. Snow White fires wide. She does it on purpose. Come on. Just shoot back. Their horses skitter and the sound of seven hammers rocking back clicks up like cards shuffling. But they don't crease her. Snow White She screams through the rain for no point but to scare them though they don't scare and her hollering puts them in a for-giving mood, seeing as how they're hollerers themselves. Snow White wants to cry but her but she's dried out. She's got ruby dust and grime and the shit of the deep earth in her and that's about it. She looks up at the rain and noise comes out of her. Ain't screaming or crying or talking, just noise, noise out of her blood. The rain fills up her mouth like milk.

This is what the women of Oh-Be-Joyful say to Snow White.

Ain't you cut a swell.

Stow that nail-pounder or we'll blow you under the earth.

Come you from the scrap of Crow Nation over the hill?

A white girl alone is trouble on everything she touches. Ask us. Don't we know.

Don't you look at her like that, Bang-Up. Can't bring her home. Can't risk it. She'll open the door to anyone who hap-pens by and wonder why we ever locked it.

Hush it. What's the place for if not half rain-drowned wildcats.

Come to town. I'll pour you a pair of overalls myself and we'll split up your sorrows seven ways between us.

Snow White
Puts a Saddle
On Her Back

ocklebur sits Snow White down in a tin bathtub, peels her out: first the road comes off, then the gunfight, then the mine and then the running, the old mirror and the boardwalk, the bunched up tiredness of everything and all of her. The water's black. Snow White frowns so deep you couldn't dig her out with a shovel, lets the bath burn her, lets the lady brush her hair like it matters.

The water's warm. No ice melting inside her. It just smells like river and the kettle. Cocky don't say anything and that's as good as love right about now.

Snow White stops doing and lets the rest do for awhile. Lets Old Ephraim feed her bunny and beans, lets Little Mab put her in some poor dead bastard's kit. Snow White declines the mirror. Mirrors are an ugly business. She's done seeing herself.

Is she fixing to stay? She talks less than a lump of dough I'll tell you what.

For awhile Snow White lets Bang-Up Jackson give her a bed. It's a little house but it's stalwart. Snow White sleeps all the time. Lies on the bed with her eyes shut and doesn't move. A moth lands on her nose and she don't so much as twitch. It's easy not to get up. Not to move. But Bang-Up won't let that go.

We live rough but we live useful and I don't support no pillow rancher. You ain't no woodstove; you can't just squat in the middle of my house and stew.

Witch Hex has been at the pine gulch with her axe. She started up the night they brought Snow White over the mountain. Without saying a word on it, the Mainer with shoulders like skin drums has stacked up pile of wood and nails north of the big frying pan in the middle of the village. Snow White will be expected to build when she's feeling straightened. Witch Hex always says building is medicine for free.

Snow White likes the work more than she expects. She don't talk to anyone much. There's a logic to a house. Though she's no great shakes and hers will win no prizes, Snow White's house will hold still in the wind. She whacks at wood with her hammer and shoots beaver for Ephie's pan and combs Charming til he glows. At night she makes that not-talking not-screaming not-crying noise down the gulch until the owls light out for friendlier digs. She can't stop. It feels so good to get empty.

Little Mab and Astolaine help the raising of her walls and the roof will go on soon. Snow White dreams about the dude and sleeps next to Bang-Up Jackson, who holds her when she shakes but lets go before she wakes up. In her dream, the dude looks like Mr. H. He wants to play cards. He calls and shows all court cards. Hands her the Queen of Spades. He says to her: *take this heart and put it in a wooden box.* Then the dude isn't the dude but the coyote in his cage in her old zoo. He spits out the body of Thompson the red fox. Howls. The noise coming out of his howl is the noise Snow White makes at night. The coyote says: *it looks like a choice but it isn't.*

There's other women in camp Snow White doesn't know to look at, and they don't wear the horse skulls and breastplates but on Sunday for the services run by Woman Without a Name, who's put her thumb down on the notion of Snow White hunting up her mama's folk. *Don't you carve your wounds on them. Ain't no place for you but here. You're grown—crooked and backbent, but grown—and it's time to stop hanging your heart on your mother.*

Snow White says ok but she can't do it. Some loads are too heavy to put down.

Bang-Up says everybody's got to contribute. Turns out a camp is just like a body; you work all day just to keep it alive. A couple of sisters keep up a watch for anyone sniffing too close to Joyful: one day, one night. They don't so much as look at anyone else. Only see each other at dusk and dawn, sharing out bread and beaver tail in the bloody light. Old Epharim allows as how their daddy was a Pennsylvania preacher of the tongues-and-snakes sort, and on account of the Bible taking a frown to the gossip of women, he cut out their tongues. The sisters have three guns each and Snow White has heard them humming to each other. She likes the sound.

Snow White does what she knows to do. She brings in meat. All day and night blood and gristle. Goes into the forest and kills what will let her kill it. First time she kills a fox she doesn't talk for three days. She plants onions in the earth like chunks of bone and keeps the bears off with Rose Red, marking the perimeter at dawn. Some of the girls want to get into the cattle business and Snow White allows that she could be talked into it. She likes the idea of a lot of beasts together under the old, cold sky, snorting and smelling like dirt. She likes the redness and realness of meat, the work of turning a deer into another day living in this world. She could do it to a cow. No sweat.

She builds a door strong and bolted and the house is creaky but sound for sleeping. But Bang-Up's bed is hard to leave and Snow White doesn't much care to. She goes to hers in the morning and comes back for supper. One day. One night.

Time trots along. Snow White chases her own tail.

On good nights, when Bang-Up falls asleep holding her hand, Snow White dreams she's a dog. She gets to sleep by the fire and eat bones and instead of talking she just howls until the moon breaks. It's a good dream.

Red Deer Sneaks Up on
Snow White

Someone else has Snow White's trail. He moves by night so no one can clap eye on him, sound alarm and call a preacher out of bed. He don't rightly know why it is he wants to find her so damn bad, but he does. It's like he's magnetized to her. But fact is he's never met the girl.

He has a name but he can't keep it in his head. People say it and it rolls off. He thinks of himself as Deer Boy and that's on account of his being half deer—he runs after the girl with black hair on long, backbent brown legs with white stripes down to the hoof. In spring he'll knock fuzz off his antlers. Rest of him's man enough but Deer Boy knows he ain't right. If he set foot in church the font would set to boiling.

Deer Boy knows he's a disappointment to his mother. He don't know how he was supposed to turn out but he knows he's got wrongness all over him, knows when she looks at him she gets so angry the walls try to get clear of her. Deer Boy wishes he knew how he got the way he is but some things are just past him. He remembers the first time he saw Snow White and likes that memory so he figures he'll live in it and that works for a little while: a sad girl on the other side of a mirror, standing next to someone so pretty it hurts to look at her, someone who looks like his mother but sharper, more real, like a lion to a housecat.

Deer Boy used to live in a perfect place. He drank silver milk from his mother and she sang nice backward nonsense songs and the sun was so soft and yellow you could spread it on toast. He didn't have deer parts back then and he got big real fast. He even had hopes of being handsome, a real shot at it. Then when he was just about grown up, the painful pretty woman came to the mirror and held out her hands to Deer Boy. She was holding a big, dripping, bloody heart, a heart so red and dark it feared him terrible. The heart came through the mirror like a red dark train and his mother went up like gas and Deer Boy lost the perfect place so fast it was like dying cold.

When he squeezed through the mirror and into the world owned by the painful woman, he was Deer Boy and he had hooves and spotted red fur on his legs and what could you do. He also spoke backwards from other folk on this side of the mirror, which upset just about everyone. His new mother did not sing nonsense songs and she had no milk for him. She howled and ran her bloody fingers over his face, kissing him and being angry at the same time.

She'd been tricked. There'd been a methodology and some part had sproinged. Deer Boy understood that he was a cake that failed to rise. He thought that'd be all right. Mothers forgive, that's what they do. She looked just like his mother. It'd be like that perfect place again once she cooled off. He could run so terrible fast, after all. It was a nice aspect in a son.

But she only said she'd fix him and over time Deer Boy came to an understanding that this meant finding Snow White. His mother owed somebody a heart. Snow White was the broken wheel in the works of his being born. Once he'd got fixed, he could see his father. Once he got fixed he could have that big house by the sea. Once he got fixed he'd get to crawl into his mother's arms and her kisses would just be kisses and leave no blood behind. He couldn't square the reason behind it all, exactly, but the painful pretty woman was his mother, somehow, the source of his mother, and no new one was going to show up and look kindly on his legs and his speaking and his singing.

If he ever meant to get back into that perfect place, Deer Boy was gonna have to run Snow White down.

Snow White
Dances with Prairie Dog

itch Hex draws the straw and goes knocking on Snow White's hickory door. Snow White opens it quick and she's hardly got anything on, it's so damnably hot and she's coating the floor with some nice whitewash Old Ephraim stewed up out of hill chalk. Snow White's full splattered with it.

"See, that's the trouble," says Witch Hex Watson. "The trouble's that door and you're gonna meet it sooner or later. We all do."

Snow White turns the floor into winter. Back and forth sweeps her brush.

"Listen, girl, I came to tell you that life is stupid. It just pulls the same shit over and over. Sometimes you think you can make it come out different, but you can't. You're in a story and the body writing it is an asshole. You had to know that, given the action. The story you're in tells you like firing a gun. And because you're in a story and stuck with the plum stupidity of being alive, I'm here to tell you not to go around opening your nice new door. Because eventually someone comes for us. All of us. Sometimes it's a husband who forgot why he beat you into running to begin with, sometimes it's a boss or a pimp looking to lay money on your belly, sometimes it's your mother come to drag you home. And pretty much we all open the door to them because it's natural. But we got a nice thing going here. Life's still stupid but we got free of story out here under the beeches and the Big Dipper. We had enough of it, of things happening one after another and no end in sight. Of reversals and falling in love and tragic flaws and by God if I see another motif in my business I will shoot it dead. The stories that happen to people like us aren't worth my back teeth. So if you want it you can have a nice life here. You can wake up next to Jackson til the end of days and the raising of the glorious dead. You can eat squirrel pancakes out of Ephie's pan and watch the moon go up and down. It's a kind of magic, but then most things are. But story is an eager fucking beaver and someday soon someone will come knocking for you and you'd better just say *no thank you* is all I'm saying. Whatever's on the other side of that *let me in* will burn you hollow and lick the ash for the last of you. The worst thing in the world is having to go back to the dark you shook off."

Snow White turns the floor to milk. Back and forth she sweeps her brush.

"My babies came knocking for me," whispers Witch Hex Watson. "Near grown up and crying for their ma. *We never believed what they said, no how. We brought you combs for your hair and ribbons for your dresses. Come home, Papa's not mad. Come back and be Mary-Grace again. Witch Hex ain't no kind of name for somebody's mother.* And I watched them crying with snot in their faces and I couldn't say no to my boys, I opened my door and everything they had for me was tainted because the land of Used-To-Be is just full of ghosts starving for your breath. What's east is hungry. What's west is hard. Just hunker down. Let it pass you by."

Snow White turns the floor to bone. Back and forth.

Snow White
Calls the Animals Together for a Meeting

ut in the forest, Snow White finds a kit whose mother probably sizzled up on Ephie's pan some night that week. He's half-blind and barely as big as her hand. Little fella mews and yelps when he sees her. Not-screaming, not-crying. He's afraid but he's hungry. Any girl in a storm.

The kit is red. Snow White takes him home. He sleeps next to her stove and pisses in the corners. His piss smells hot and sour. He bites her. Snow White bites back. They understand each other.

A while later, Snow White sees a bear in the woods. She's old and stiff. She has a patch of bald on her rump where she's worried the fur away. The bear follows Snow White and watches her dress a raccoon. The blood makes the dirt damp and black. Snow White does not shoot the bear, even though she could. The bear is very slow. They never come too close but they like to look at each other. The bear grabs a fish out of the crick and the way she glances at Snow White it's like the old girl wants to be praised. Snow White leaves trout guts for her and keeps the red fox from gobbling them up.

The trees stand green as summer, all in a line.

The red fox gets big. He likes to keep watch with the night-sister and her three guns. But when thunderstorms belly up to the Joyful bar, he comes running to Snow White. He pisses on her bed. She knows that he means to indicate that he considers it his bed. That's fine.

Snow White stops letting her noise out at night. It fears the bear too much.

Red Deer
and the Bird from Heaven

eer Boy is not a tracker. His deer half is the wrong half. His human nose is as dumb as anyone's. Besides, deer have the drive to run away, not seek out. They get hunted, they do not hunt. If he had his mother's brains, he might have called up Chicago and got his own dude to stand him to the trail. But he didn't get her mind within mind in the parental bargain and he's chasing blind, running on the fuel of his want. He's playing his father's tune, but he doesn't know it.

Deer Boy has often cogitated upon the subject of what he will do if he finds her. There is not much else to think about. He imagines her. He builds her out of his memory. He runs up to her on puts his hands up on the glass between them. Is she his sister? Some days he thinks yes, some days he thinks no. Deer Boy was born in the mirror. She looks nothing like him. But look at their hands, pressing together, ten fingers to ten fingers. They are the same. They are standing with a mirror between them. They are standing with his mother between them.

Can he cut her heart out? He tells himself yes. The answer is no.

Deer Boy wear long trousers and chaps that hide his legs. When he drinks whiskey he can almost talk straight. He plays cards and bets for information. He bets for stories. When the Ace of Hearts turns over his breath stops. It doesn't even have to be in his hand. *Johnny, you remember when that crazy half-breed bitch shot ol' pieface Hank out back, right? Those were the days. A man felt alive.*

She is a half-breed. She is like him. Deer Boy does not know what her other half is but he wonders if being split down the middle pains her like it pains him.

Deer Boy would like to meet his father. He reads about him all the time. The Dakota rush. The Colorado lode. In his mind, Deer Boy's father is made of jewels. When Deer Boy gets his legs back, his father will open up his diamond arms and gather him into the glitter. He dreams about this. On the other side of his father's crystal body, Snow White puts up her hands.

Once, Deer Boy tried to ask his mother why she didn't just leave him in the mirror. *Why am I myself and not some other boy? Why can't you love what you made?*

He spoke backwards. She didn't understand. She said: *you are my price. You are my black deal in the wood.*

Deer Boy gets so drunk in Haul-Off he has to be rolled out onto the street. It's raining dog. He stumbles up the road, his hooves sticking in the mud. The whiskey in him stands at attention. Up ahead of him he thinks he sees her, Snow White, wet and cold, her face on fire with light. She's standing in the road; a body sprawls next to her. A bullet between his eyes.

I need your heart.

She puts her hands up. Ten fingers.

I'm sorry. I need your heart.

Snow White opens her mouth. Milk flows out.

I just want to be loved. Didn't you ever want her to love you?

Snow White opens her chest like a cabinet. She takes out her heart. It is a ruby. It is dripping blood. It is dripping light. She looks at him with so much love.

Deer Boy wakes up holding his hat tender as a baby.

Snow White
and the Money Tree

It **is around** this time that Little Mab Volsky propositions Snow White. Let's us rob ourselves a bank. Easiest money this side of lying on your back, she says. When a vault busts open it's like you bust, too. That sweet. That good.

They practice in the woods.

Snow White puts a kerchief over her face and it is a red mask. Little Mab'll run the show—Snow White can just shoot up the place. They holler at the crick to lie down on its belly, double quick and no funny business. Snow White bags a jackrabbit with a white blaze on his chest like a sheriff's star. He looked at her crooked. You can't brook that kind of upfuck. They bash in a rotted stump and get it down to forty-five seconds from first thump to vault open and pillbugs rolling out like dimes.

Little Mab has this to say: "The thing to know about bank robberies is that most fellas who end up blowing dark through some poor soul with a withdrawal slip in his hand wanted to do it before they ever got in the door. They wanted to make a hole in something and fill up the hole with death. Most times the bank is empty anyways. Not too many got much these days. Folks who got unlucky business there, well, they'll put their bellies on the floor you'll forget what you came for. They're like dogs before an earthquake. Some instinct kicks them in the gut and down they go. We'll take just what we need, enough for doorknobs and seedbags and a good bull to mate to the milk cows. Enough to turn into another day in this world. We'll get Lainey to fiddle while we rob. Make it nice for them folks on the floor. Ain't nothing to be done in this life but you can't make it nicer for them you do it to."

Snow White can see it clear as day. She'll land in that bank like a hammer. Rose Red will dance in her hand. She still has a few pearls left. Little Mab will holler and laugh like a fairy on fire. She'll do a jig in front of the safe like she could cozen it into shedding its cover for her. Snow White can hear Astolaine playing her violin by the door. The customers will all start crying when they hear her tune. Crying out of the same place that told them to lay their head on the cool bank stone.

Snow White wants to shoot the ceiling, the walls, the glass. She wants to put a hole in something, too. She just doesn't want to fill it up again.

Snow White
and Yellow Jacket
Get Turned Back
at the River

Bang-Up puts the nix on the bank plan. Banks are like little bits of Washington poking up everywhere. Banks are the law.

"Now, we've gone to all this trouble to truss up our lives nice and tight with no space for the bad to come in. Why you want to go throwing open the door?"

Red Deer
Learns a Trade

eer Boy runs out of scratch somewhere in Wyoming. He starts showing his legs for a dollar in a cathouse. While ranch-hands wait for their friends to finish up. A dollar for a hoof, three for the whole leg. The food is good. There are mirrors everywhere. Deer Boy sees himself all night every night. He looks for the perfect world in them but it's just him in there.

The girls treat him real sweet. Not like you'd treat a beau—Deer Boy is not husband material. But they're in the same line of work. One dollar for a peek. Three for the whole show.

One of the cats gets marriage proposals every night. She's got red hair and a pretty voice on her. Deer Boy hears the men begging her through the walls. Through the mirrors.

Give me your heart.

PART V

Snow White Comes
to Life Three Times

Snow White
Gets Shot with a Pine Tree

It **happens just** as autumn's coming on red and sharp.

Bang-Up Jackson's gone south to haggle over jerseys and a lump of tourmaline the shape and weight of a human heart. Witch Hex is drunk down the gulch and letting the sun sop her further. Woman Without a Name is burning ash for soap by the creek. Everyone's minding theirs.

Old Epharim sees her come, but nobody and nothing troubles that old bear. She stirs her stew. Badger, beans, and black honeycomb.

Snow White hears a knock and she thinks she knows what's up, thinks she knows to turn away whatever's rapping. But she's not ready and she could never be. Out the window stands her mother. Not Mrs. H. No, this is Gun That Sings. Older, grey in the pomp, face carved like someone meant to write something there and never finished. But it's her. Snow White sees her own face. Her dark eyes. Her mouth red as feeding. Her hurt laid out like leather. It's not a fair fight. Not even a whiff. Some things a girl has in her to say no to and some things cut her down before she knows she's gone. Sure, some twiggy, thorny snap in her says: *no, this is awry, this is a bent thing,* in that place that tells her to belly up to the floor before anyone's even shadowed the doorframe. But it don't matter. You can't ask why she did it, when she was warned, when she was told. The plum truth is you would too, if everything impossible stood out there saying you could be loved so perfect the past would go up like a firecracker and shatter across the dark.

Snow White grabs on to her mama and don't let go. First she's quiet like morning, then she says *mama* a couple of times, real small against that brown shoulder. Sure, Gun That Sings don't smell right—smells like a cold forest and a pool of frozen silver—but maybe that's what a mother smells like. How would she know?

"There now," says Gun That Sings. "I found you. It's all right."

"You're dead."

"What's dead but a little slower than the living? I got here. Let's you and I roll us some cigarettes and talk up the moon. I bet no one ever taught you to roll a cigarette proper."

She don't sound right either. Sounds like the wheels spinning on a slot machine, rolling up all winter.

"Remember what I said about magic and don't be so quick to call me the devil, child."

Snow White wants a mother so bad it's like a torn up body wanting blood. She knows how to roll a damned cigarette. Could teach the Tobacco King of Carolina to do it nice and tight for once. But she lets her mama show her, crushing the dried up leaves against white paper.

"I tried to find the Crow Nation. I tried to find you."

"Oh, you don't want to do that," croons Gun That Sings. "You'd be the fairest of them all. No more at home than at your father's table, all dolled up like any dress could fix you. Don't go sticking your hangdog face where it's not wanted. Ain't those poor folk been strick enough? Don't need Miss H to haul water for them, no ma'am."

Snow White takes the name like a fist. *Go inside*, her bank sense says. *She's nothing but a creature and she ain't your mama. This will go bad on you.*

Snow White takes a shaky draw on her cigarette and falls down dead.

Snow White
Breathes Lightning

Snow White comes to with Bang-Up kissing her, sucking the smoke out of her body like steam coming off a pond. Bang-Up's nearly crying which for most folks is all the way crying and it's a bad night. Coughing, throwing up black pitch like the devil's shit, Old Epharim feeding her bear broth and everyone growling her *didn't we say, didn't Hex tell you up and down, what's addled you, girl.*

When Snow White finally sleeps it's like being buried, that deep, that heavy.

You said. You said.

Snow White
Drinks the Ocean

It **happens again** when acorns start their rat-a-tat falling, like cavalry guns on the hill.

Little Mab's gone west to do a train job: coin and corn and a hunk of pearl as heavy as a human heart. She couldn't stand it, not stealing anything for so long. Cocklebur is entertaining a law-man with a taste for green stockings. Astolaine Bombast is skinning a raccoon for fur and victuals. Everyone's minding theirs.

Old Epharim sees her come, but nobody and nothing troubles that old bear. She stirs her stew. Beaver, beans, and beets as red as blood.

Snow White hears a knock and she thinks she knows what's up, thinks she knows to turn away whatever's thumping. She's not even surprised to see her mama there again, looking like nothing ever went south, like she just wanted to see her girl again. Just wanted to jaw about the weather. Door's open before Snow White can stop herself. A mother's like a poison made for only one soul. She opens the door because on the other side it's her own face looking back, it's a mirror as big as her whole life and she just wants to be saved.

"Come on, baby girl. We didn't finish our conversating. Set on the porch with me and we'll share some good whiskey. I bet no one ever taught you how to drink whiskey straight."

Snow White sits down. She knows how to drink for fuck's sake. Could teach the Scottish laird who dreamed up whiskey in his sheep pen to bolt it down and never flinch.

And this time she's got Rose Red with her.

Snow White cocks her girl and she doesn't say *who are you* or *if you play me poor I can play you back.* She just sits there with death pointed at her mother. She can feel the blood in her cheeks and her breath hitches.

"You look just like your father, staring at me like that," sneers the thing wearing the face of Gun That Sings.

Snow White swallows that like a sword. She lets the hammer click back in its place. Everything in her that's not nailed down is shaking loose.

Snow White slugs back her whiskey and falls down dead.

Snow White
Exchanges Vomit with Owl

She comes to and Bang-Up's got her fingers down her throat. The whiskey comes back up like it hates her personal, there's puke everywhere and a skunky red in her eyes. Bang-Up punches a few walls and it's a bad night. No one comes round from a thing like that looking pretty. Retching and sweating and a lump of hide in Snow White's mouth so she don't make supper of her tongue. Everyone snarling *twice means you wanted it, what's soured out in you girl, is you looking for your death or just banging into it full stupid?*

When she finally sleeps it's like drowning, that dark, that final.

I'm looking for it. I'm looking for it.

Snow White
Swallows the Earth

It happens again when the snow starts riding the wind, not fallen yet but ashing the air.

Everyone's in camp this time. They see it happen. Even Bang-Up. But they don't interfere. Everyone's minding theirs. Only so much you can do to keep a body going when it's bent on blowing town. They all see her come.

Old Epharim stirs her stew. Fox meat and coyote bones and deer hearts black as secrets.

Snow White doesn't wait. In the bank of her whole self she's already laid out on the floor. But it's not her mama come to shoot the place up.

It's Mrs. H.

Older, white freezing the edges of her hair, lines in her face like someone meant to scar her forever but didn't have the heart to finish up. But it's her. Snow White sees a face she knows and fears and loves in an ugly, bunched up way. A family way.

It's not a fair fight.

Mrs. H is holding a basket of apples. They look real nice. Snow White keeps her mouth shut—it's all said anyway. She just looks at her stepmother holding her death bag of Puritan magic between them like they don't both know what's going to happen.

And yet. Mrs. H falters. Snow White is the best draw going and her stare punches a hole at point blank. She aims to fill it this time.

"Everything in this world requires a heart in trade," Mrs. H whispers. "There's no such thing as a good bargain."

Yeah. That's about the speed of it.

Mrs. H pulls out a deck of cards. Thompson's fox-teeth show on the back of the seven of spades. She offers Snow White the cut, fair as fair as fair.

Snow White don't take it.

Snow White reaches out and grabs an apple from the bag. She bites into it and never looks away from Mrs. H, from the crevice of her, and this is a suicide we're watching, full faith and knowledge.

Snow White swallows that piece of sweetness and falls down dead.

Her mother catches her.

PART VI

Snow White
Rides a Star

Snow White
Is Carried By Turtle

What **happens** **to** the West happens to Snow White, which is to say they both turn into jokes. They both get told so often they become pantomime. And then worse.

Oh-Be-Joyful don't last much past Montana Territory unterritorying and stating up. But you never leave a girl behind. They join up with a wild west show and tour flat-dead towns on scrub-dust rivers. Not the big show, Bill's show, but one nearly as good. They earn their dinners. The trick shots Little Mab and Bang-Up pull off look just like magic. What Woman Without a Name does with a horse would shame anyone who dared call himself a cowboy which truth be told is not too many people anymore.

And they have a pair of aces. A curiosity unequaled. It goes in the freak show because no one knows what else to do with it, and Boss Jake says it gives him the crawling creeps.

A little while back someone else showed up asking after work, though everybody but the lions knew he was just looking for their funny little curiosity. That kid was a much better get than the old box anyway, with those deer legs that could outrun a horse. Spends most of his nights in the freak tent with the box, talking to it like it can talk back. Talking funny. Maybe it's French or something. Boss Jake knows he's got a genuine cryptozoo on his hands, so he lets Deer Boy do whatever he wants. Only he says it *cripplezoo* because Boss Jake ain't too bright and learned his words off his daddy's bad mouth.

If you pay your nickel you can see it easy enough. Read the nice red sign up there: *The Glass Gunslinger.* And there she is: a glass box wrapped up in some old mangy coyote pelts and inside it there's a girl. Sort of pretty, or she would have been if she hadn't run herself so hard when she could run. Jake reckons she's Choctaw or Cree or something and he don't care when Woman Without a Name tells him she's half-Crow and half-son-of-a-bitch.

Don't look Snow White to me nohow.

Bang-Up Jackson makes sure the gunslinger's hair looks nice before shows, crosses her arms over her chest with a big crazy pistol all pigged up in jewels in one hand and a long hog-sticker rifle in the other. Keeps her face clean. Keeps the flies off.

The gunslinger isn't dead, but she don't move and she barely breathes, so in summer she don't smell too nice and the flies come singing. That's when the Joyful girls—the furies, Jake calls them—take her out of her box and wash her in whatever's handy. They let the Deer Boy help and the way he holds her head you'd think he'd married her before she got put in that box.

Old Epharim catches Deer Boy kissing the gunslinger once. Standing there with the box open and crying while he kissed her red, red lips. Nothing and no one troubles the old bear. She let them alone, though she didn't feel right on it considering he was a stranger and Bang-Up would have both those pretty deer legs bust out if she knew. But what does it matter? Been twenty years now and Snow White don't look a day older, don't ever sit up and ask for whiskey in her coffee, don't do nothing but beat her heart and work her breath.

Deer Boy kisses Snow White again.

She doesn't wake up.

Snow White
and Red Deer Contend for a Piece of Meat

eer Boy stands over the glass gun-slinger one night in autumn. Everything smells like woodsmoke.

He puts his hands on the glass of her box. Leans in. Deer Boy can see himself in the glass. He can see her through him.

Deer Boy's heard his mother's sick back home. The lunger, maybe. But she's old, so it doesn't matter what it is. When she coughs it comes up red as apples. It has occurred to him that he should go to her. If he brought her what she wanted, she might heal up. Might look at him and say: *what a good boy.*

Deer Boy brought a knife with him. He holds it between himself and Snow White.

I need your heart.

He opens the glass. Snow White is warm. He ran so far and now he runs alongside her. Keeping pace. Keeping time.

He doesn't try to understand things anymore. Deer Boy just loves like a light bulb and he never goes off.

"It looks like a choice," he says to her soft as falling, "between you and me. But it isn't."

When the words come out they run backwards.

Deer Boy drags the knife over his chest. He is giving her his heart. He is exchanging a deer's heart for a girl's heart. If hers would fix him, his will fix her. He knows it. She isn't his sister. She is his sister.

Deer Boy sees her eyelids move. He thinks he sees it. He's sure he sees it.

Boss Jake hauls him back yelling for help. Hauls him off of her and Deer Boy is crying, he is begging her to wake up. *She's dead, she's dead, you can come back now.*

The furies clean him up. He didn't cut deep enough. Never could. No damage done. Snow White don't move a whisper.

Deer Boy's blood seeps into her white calfskins like snow.

Snow White
and the Story
of Death

Well, there's only two ways this can end. Snow White wakes up; Snow White sleeps forever. Maybe that's her thing. She's always waking up and always sleeping at the same time all the time, so fast you can't see the blur.

Maybe she never wakes up. More likely than anything else, really. You can't kiss a girl into anything.

Snow White becomes an object. Barnum buys or steals her from Jakob's show and she cools her heels with the Fiji Mermaid in perpetuity. A medical museum. A private collector with a scar on his chest. Maybe someday Snow White's cells get scraped and stored for some researcher to kiss alive in a decade, a century, when they get around to it. When they have time.

She dreams of the mine. Of rubies hanging in the dark like antibodies. She dreams of her mother singing to her like a gun. She dreams of her mother when she was a girl, and didn't know the future. If you want to know.

You know, there's this old story. It says Coyote took his heart and cut it in half. He put one half right at the tip of his nose and the other half at the end of his tail. He did this so no one could catch him at his mischief. The two halves of his heart would fly off in separate directions, each doing whatever it pleased, and if anyone said to one half of his heart: *you have done a wicked thing!* the other half would say: *what the hell you talking about, I was over here the whole time!*

Alive and dead, alive and dead. Both happening so fast you can't see the blur. It doesn't matter which. The live girl carries around the deadness she worked on all those years. The dead girl holds on to that wick of living that's still green in there. It flips back and forth forever like a trick ace. *Thump, thump, thump* in the night as a girl sits up and lays down again.

Come on. Pick one. Pick a path and hit the briars.

Snow White
Holds Up the Sky

T_hump, thump, thump._
_One thing I have learned about running away is
that once you start there is no end to it._

Open, shut. Alive, dead. Sooner or later you choose. This
is what happens.

Snow White dreams about old red Thompson the fox and
the spinning trees on her slots, red and gold and green and
white. She dreams about the seagull with a bullet through its
eye. If you want to know.

She dreams Mrs. H palms up that deck again. And this
time she takes the cut. Aces high.

And all right, okay, one day she wakes up. It's a hundred
years, a hundred and ten, maybe some change. Stowed away
in some attic in Iowa where Jakob's Exhibition of Wildness
and Wonder petered out. She wakes up because there was
flooding all over town that spring and the current washed
that house clean off its stones. Snow White wakes up when

her glass box crunches against an elm tree and goes accordion shaped. Or maybe it was just time. Some clock ticked out inside her. Four old trees spinning up to spring.

There's glass in her hair. In her palms.

Search and Rescue airlifts Snow White and half the town clear of the whitewater and nobody thinks much of it. A man with a crew cut treats her for shock. He asks how many fingers. Who's President.

Snow White sees a taxidermied horse float down Beech Street and she knows it's Charming. There's a piece of glass in her nipple, poking out like a drop of milk that never fell. Right over her heart.

Snow White gets a social security card. She gets a job building houses out in California. Picks oranges. Doesn't talk about herself. Never did. If you press her she'll say she lost everything in the flood and she supposes that's true. She goes to see the castle by the sea and it's a museum now. Pictures on the wall: the Mr. Buttons. Miss Enger. Mr. H.

Mrs. H.

The pictures are black and white and Snow White finds no answers there or any comfort either. They just look like dead people and that's what they are. Her room is labeled: *guest quarters* and she supposes that's true, too. Up in the hills, the boardwalk is not open to visitors. Under construction. Renewal efforts funded by a grant from the state. Excellent example of turn-of-the-century follies.

In the forest Snow White sees a red fox. He looks at her for a long time. She tosses him an apple. Little fellow sniffs but he knows better. Good boy. Good boy.

Snow White likes the open sky. It's the same as it ever was. Fire and cold. Long empty spaces between the stars, stars like towns getting their grips into a big black country.

Oh-Be-Joyful. Haul-Off. Blue Coffin. There's red up there like rubies in a mine.

Snow White gets a doctorate in physics though it takes her about fifteen years. She sleeps with a couple of lab partners but it's pretty uninspiring stuff. She meets a history professor. He walks with an odd wobble. His students make fun of the way he talks—but they make fun of her drawl, too. Snow White does not think much of students. She waves at the professor when she passes by his classroom. Waves through the little glass window. He puts up his hand to hers. Snow White decides to take him to dinner. Find out his story. When she has time. There's so much to do.

The telescopes open up to the sky like gardenias at a wedding.

Whoever's left standing has won.

Snow White discovers a new pulsar out in the Horsehead Nebula. She listens to it through machines that reflect her face.

Thump, thump, thump.

Talking mirrors on every wall.

Thump, thump, thump.

Snow White's pulsar shakes the night sky like iron shoes dancing.